Translated from
the Spanish by
Will Vanderhyden

SPIRITUAL

CHOREOGRAPHIES

CARLOS LABBÉ

OPEN LETTER
LITERARY TRANSLATIONS FROM THE UNIVERSITY OF ROCHESTER

First edition, 2019
All rights reserved

Library of Congress Cataloging-in-Publication Data: Available.
ISBN-13: 978-1-940953-97-7 / ISBN-10: 1-940953-97-9

This project is supported in part by the New York State Council on the Arts with the support of Governor Andrew M. Cuomo and the New York State Legislature.

 Council on
the Arts

Printed on acid-free paper in the United States of America.

Text set in Dante, a mid-20th-century book typeface designed by Giovanni Mardersteig. The original type was cut by Charles Malin.

Design by N. J. Furl

Open Letter is the University of Rochester's nonprofit, literary translation press:
Dewey Hall 1-219, Box 278968, Rochester, NY 14627

www.openletterbooks.org

PRAISE FOR
CARLOS LABBÉ

"Begins to fuck with your head from its very first word."

—Toby Litt

"What we encounter in *Loquela* is a skillful unmaking—complete with diary excerpts, missives from beyond the grave and an invented barn-burning manifesto on a literary movement, 'Corporalism,' which seeks to breathe life into the 'corpse' of literature—that manages to offer new ways of thinking about what the novel can do."

—Laird Hunt, *L.A. Times*

"Labbé wreaks havoc on narrative rules from the start and keeps doing it."

—*Bookforum*

"*Loquela* is drenched in the spirit of experimentality, dry and absurd humor, strangeness, and intrigue."

—Simone Wolff, *Bookslut*

"*Navidad & Matanza* could be the hallucinogenic amalgamation of a César Aira plot with setting and characters conceived by Bolaño if written using Oulipo-style constraints. . . . With ample imagination and commanding style, *Navidad & Matanza* certainly marks Labbé as a young author from whom we ought to anticipate great, fascinating things to come."

—Jeremy Garber, Powell's Books

ALSO BY
CARLOS LABBÉ

Loquela
Navidad & Matanza

For Inti, Mónica Ramón Ríos,
and the Labbé Jorqueras.

In memory of Caries, Ex Fiesta,
Tornasólidos, Triple Turbante,
and the Costa Rica Space Program

SPIRITUAL

CHOREOGRAPHIES

The choreography needs someone to witness its movements.

I am he.

I am he, the other, she, you, they.

He played the harmonica with his nose, pulled out his handkerchief and blew until all the pollution of the capital was expelled from his lungs in one transparent color. He finger-tapped his flat chest like a kultrun, *gargling to imitate a harp.*

He thought he'd be able to escape to his tree when he could not longer bear the smog of the city.

I, on the other hand, now that I have no nostrils with which to inhale or exhale, want a melody of bows and strings and stones to still be raining down from all five fingers, onto this skin, stretched across this orthopedic wheelchair, when the sun rises.

On the table, in the sunlight, there should've been some kind of animal, not this screen where each movement of my pupil writes a soundless name.

13.
CORRECTION

The choreography needs audience, needs someone to witness its movements. The damp twilight wind slammed shut the kitchen window. She was cutting leeks at the sink when the sash colliding with the frame startled her; the shards of glass turned to fragments on the floor a few meters away. The shock made her jerk the knife across the back of her left hand. When the boy entered dressed in pajamas, hair mussed—mother, what was that? his question—she was standing there, staring at the shape of that small wound under the stream of water, as if it reminded her of some profound, lost thing. One sound, two, a counterpoint, the dark night looking out at waves, she thought. And then there was just her blood, staining the water in the sink. She brought her hand to her mouth so she wouldn't ruin the vegetable with her foul taste.

"Go shower, we're eating soon. And bring him down," she told the boy.

Ten minutes later they were all sitting in silence around the kitchen table. She had to quicken her breathing and open her eyes: the little wound on her hand kept her from concentrating, pulsing in the dark, like the double of another wound on the palm of the hand of a man who in her memory recoiled from a seashell, from a broken bottle, tears and sweat; she was naked, on the wave-packed sand, wet. I was another person back then, she thought.

"Life here begins many times," the vocalist blurted out unexpectedly from his wheelchair.

He did so without solemnity, but with a voice not his own.

It was a little unsettling, according to the doctors, his neurological damage rendered speech impossible, but that was the third time in a year he'd spoken during meditation. For an instant, the boy opened his eyes too; he and his mother exchanged a glance just as a draft swept in through the broken window and caused a distant door—the bathroom door, she guessed—to slam. Then they heard the beep, beep, beep of the alarm being deactivated at the front entrance. It was the other, returning from the recording studio. He came in carrying a paper bag, set it down in the middle of the table, and went into the kitchen. Reaching out her fingers, she removed a still-warm roll from the bag and tore it open, scanning with her eyes, in vain, for the jam. The other shut the refrigerator with his foot, sat down; he grabbed the jar of jam and set it beside her plate— she gave him a grateful smile—and turned to the vocalist, offering him a sip of the beer he held in his hand.

Then the other raised the can and made a toast:

"Bless Him. I finished writing the bloody score today."

The boy pinched an unlit cigarette between his lips as he applauded. The movement of his hands knocked over the milk carton, which, striking the floor, bounced back up and collided with the jar of jam. Suddenly irritated, she couldn't take her eyes off the can of beer as she attempted to clean the floor with a spoon. The other brought his hands together and bent down beside her.

"The Man wanted to tell me something last night, I'm sure of it," the boy blurted out.

The vocalist tried to grimace through his paralysis.

"Was the show any good?" she asked.

"It's been proven: The Man is the greatest baritone in the history of humanity, Mother. His shows are always perfect."

"That's why he's in the bubblegum music."

The other burst out laughing at his own comment. She, all the while, watched her son speak, but couldn't understand what he was saying. Were they speaking in Chezungun again to mess with her, to exclude her? All she heard was laughter and—it's absurd, she said to herself, we're miles from the ocean—the sound of waves breaking on the beach, swelling with wind and rain. Another spark in her memory: the beach's thick sand clinging to her thighs as she spread her legs, the other's alcoholic stench on the nape of her neck, his moan in the dark: leave us alone.

"I pushed through the crowd right up to the front, seriously. And there I am, transfixed, face to face with The Man, modulating the final guitar solo with the vocoder implanted in one of his molars. Then he sees me, I'm sure of it. He sees me and wants to tell me something, something only he knows, something for my ears alone."

"My dearest, dearest lad," the other sighed under his breath. "Do not forget the stage's bright lights are there to blind the performers just enough."

She carried the plates and cups to the dishwasher as the volume of the conversation rose. According to the boy, the fact that The Man was the first clone to ever produce positive sales numbers for the record company proved nothing in terms of his musical refinement, nor did it provide any credible proof as to whether or not he was capable of feeling emotions when he sang.

"Haven't you ever seen a stranger's face pass quickly by a window, the face of a stranger to whom you must impart some important thing, a face that never comes entirely into focus, but that you just have to speak to? I swear that's what happened to The Man when he saw me."

She decided to leave them to their discussion and take the vocalist in his wheelchair to their bedroom. She thought she might purchase a *Quyasullu* film for the four of them to watch while they ate dessert. She helped prop him up in the bed, brought a few pillows in from the living room to support his back. When she gave him the remote control, he gripped her hand, his eyes fixing on that little wound, already beginning to heal. She wanted to say, to ask him one, two, three times the same question about the words he'd babbled during meditation: if, after all these weeks correcting the book about The Band on his screen, he could use his voice again, if something had made him say what he'd said, and to what end. Then the wind blew, causing another draft to slam another door. A door somewhere in the apartment. The front door? she wondered.

The choreography needs melody, the melody I can now only hear in one ear.

He, the boy, wanted to play the part of the young macho warrior and not humanity's savior.

He wanted to be the liberator and not the vocalist in a band.

I am he, and yet. No more. This useless body that once leapt across stages.

All those lives come together on this page and now it's only possible for me to quietly write with my eyelids about what isn't a lie, in the margin of this little volume of autobiographical fiction, on the table before me, in place of some unknown animal, bleeding out in the sun at the old mother's feet, the kawellu and the goats, the chicken and the tree, my brother and me.

I am he. The Band. Nothing more.

12.
CORRECTION

The choreography needs melody. And the theremin section wove together more than twenty voices. The drum machine accelerated to the rhythm of the piano chords and the double bass announced a silence that was followed by the recorded sound of a busy signal in the background. The lights flashed with the first words of the silhouette, the figure, the sweaty face that emerged from the fog. He opened his arms and dropped to his knees to sing the song of a woman who traveled the world with her terrorist cell, freeing animals from zoos, until she was caught and sentenced to life in a prison. That song had topped commercial sales charts for eighty weeks straight, before even one photo of The Band appeared on screens or in magazines. A roar erupted from the crowd of five thousand imperial kids, falling down drunk after three days of celebrating an immigrant woman being elected president. The girl who played the drum machine saw all of this from her corner of the stage; the tiny hairs on her arms stood on end. She saw how the vocalist's hard eyes fixed on a girl in the audience as she climbed onto the stage, how something changed in him when that same girl tore off her T-shirt and, like an offering, threw it at her idol, before letting herself fall back into the arms of the bouncers, swallowed by the crowd, fainting away. Likewise, she saw the shirt in his hands, how he let the microphone drop, and without turning back, walked to the dressing room, though the other tried to push him back onstage. The girl's T-shirt was blue and printed with a cross and his name, in place of the baroque *Inri*.

The choreography needs a rhythm, a rhythm that isn't moving.

I am he.

Before tossing out ten possible false names, before proposing titles, I dilate my pupil to transplant someone else's words into the beginning of this volume of autobiographical fiction:

"It's the libretto of a musical piece and some unspoken dialogues, a beyond-the-text that's nonetheless of utmost importance when it comes to reading it and that's not why it doesn't occupy the fundamental place on the page.

"Don't substitute voices.

"Don't anticipate them; don't try to express them or metamorphose them into writing.

"It's not the story of a journey, not a spiritual treatise.

"The choreography simply supplies a set of procedures and practices related to experiences that aren't described or explained, that don't entirely enter the text, and whose representation doesn't aspire to in any way, for it posits them as its own exteriors, assuming the form of an oral dialogue between the one who writes and the one who reads, or a silent history of the relationship between what goes unuttered and its two guardians."

Meanwhile, these eyelids grow heavy.

11.
CORRECTION

The choreography needs a rhythm. And the girl who later played the drum machine in The Band had asked her parents for a drum set three times, in vain; she stopped studying, the arguments got insufferable. One afternoon, she left school, walked to a bus stop, and took a bus into the city, then another to the capital, and from there, another to the port. For decades, she refused to visit her parents—who wept for her every night—but she never forgot her bedroom in that house, the soft bed with hand-woven blankets where for hours she lay, staring up at the Roneo-paper poster where the vocalist appeared, facing the camera and, simultaneously, in profile, face made up like a violet, teeth and eyes purple.

Two years later, she met him. In the embassy bathroom, at a gala hosted by the other's father. She strolled in through the garden of the well-guarded diplomatic headquarters, as if it were one of the suburban lawns of her youth; the security didn't question her and the dogs roaming the grounds failed to pick up her scent. The other never took his eyes off her. He, on the other hand, was passed out on the bathroom floor. She kissed him awake, splashed water on his face, told him she was his one and only fan.

Years before, she'd traveled as an exchange student to his home country. She'd had the good fortune of being hosted by a self-proclaimed devoutly religious family, who lived in a mountain-top mansion only accessible by car and, since she didn't have her driver's license, she passed the time reading books she took from the enormous library that the head of the house maintained in his private study, along with a collection of seashells, capped bottles, and locked drawers. She liked to stay up to watch, on the TV in her room, a music-video show on a local channel. And on one of those late nights she was mesmerized by the only recorded show of one of his previous bands. Though there were seventeen musicians on the stage, she only had eyes for the vocalist, for his moustache, his yellow bikini, and his rubber boots.

The choreography needs pause and movement.

I'm only paralyzed to the person who sees me in this chair, not to the person who looks for my eyes and fails to find them.

When I open them the previous sentence is corrected.

I am he, learning to follow the old mother across the hill where once were various species of trees that no longer exist.

She's dictating a series of words to him in the language that cannot have a name, so he'll forget them on his way somewhere and remember them as soon as he gets there. And so, only when he lies down on his back and looks up will he know if he's come to the place where the boughs lace together to form arches, doorways, gates, gyres, tunnels, keyholes, and arms.

He, who is I, realizes—when the explosions drive him up the tree and he finds the old mother riddled with the bullets of the company's security, the company that owns all this paper—that there's no such thing as tree, vocalist, keyboardist, or dancer, just a mass.

There's neither chaos nor system in this autobiographical fiction: just this mass of flesh that has be contained to remain alive, a tangle of roots that can never be exposed to the sun.

He recalls that series of proper names.

Know that I do not utter them, for to do so would erase them.

10.
CORRECTION

The choreography needs pause and movement. It was eleven in the morning. A mist fell from the gray sky; and yet, she wasn't cold, as she ran to the town cemetery.

Two hours earlier, in front of the singer-songwriter's family home, an old man in a wheelchair, whose white beard hung to his belly, had rung a bell and the mass of people wrapped in parkas, blankets, anoraks, jackets, and ponchos had bowed their heads; one couple even knelt. The air was humid and the little town had always been quiet. In the distance, a dog began to bark. A boy cried out, a young woman wept. A drunk smashed a beer bottle. A second dog joined in with a howl. Within twenty minutes, the police had already dispersed the thirty-second commemoration of the singer-songwriter's death. Over the loudspeakers, they announced that the nuclear power plant had exploded. That everyone had to evacuate. But she wouldn't break her promise. Four months ago, he'd sent her a message from the port, asking her to come meet him in that little northern town. There, he would attempt to face his fear of the audience; he would bring his guitar and pay homage to the singer-songwriter with a new song he'd written, after eight months without uttering a word.

"Fucking coward."

She tried to improve the soft consonants she used to pronounce that guttural—rabbit-like, it seemed to her—language, sitting on a gravestone, sipping from a glass one of the locals had given her. Or maybe that gravestone wasn't just any gravestone, she thought, just as she heard someone say:

"You're sitting on His tombstone, love."

The other was approaching, coming down the path through the cemetery; he shook the water out of his short hair as he spoke. He knew that the vocalist wouldn't be coming, that he had three years left to serve on his prison sentence; in any case, he'd promised him he would find a drummer for their band.

The choreography needs a stage.

He, the boy, walked behind the old mother.

He wanted to hold her hand, which was like the earth where they went together to search for stones, on the slopes of the volcano, beyond the hill; that hand seemed within reach, but it was a fist, and he didn't need the old mother to swat him away like a horsefly to keep him from taking it in his own.

I, on the other hand, deliberately trace the story of a band, which appears to have been transformed into something soft, transparent, supple, polished, comfortable, into just the right amount of light so my pupils aren't blinded and my eyelids can blink onto the screen dots and lines and marks that all of us know so none of us see.

He, the boy, said something to the old mother to make her stop, to make her delay, to make her tell him which leaves to ask for and which not to take, how long to steep them, how long to wait, looking out at the sun, about where the night went, about the circular galloping, the sowing, the path, the first blows on a freshly strung drum, about whether they would come to him in his dreams too, and give him a new tree where he could plant his feet and run through the highest boughs.

He, the boy, running through the neighborhood with his brother asked him where the old mother, the kawellu, the tree, the goats, the clay had gone. His twin looked at him with a smirk and kicked the black bags in the alley, grunting:

"If you know, why ask.

"If you have to ask it's because you don't understand where it is that we live now, that this is how you have to speak to enter the store and get a treat.

"That you have to keep moving.

"That they killed the old mother. That the old mother died alone. That your tree is now paper to wipe your ass with, that the goats were eaten by the security guards, and that the clay has been turned to sand to make the concrete of the shantytown's new streets."

He, tired, couldn't write the soundless words in the prison where they put him for killing his brother.

I, on the other hand, have just the right amount of light so that my eyelids can blink open a page that's no longer made of tree. Two hired nurses wake me if I start to drown in the hard clay.

He, the boy, stopped on the road beside the old mother, who sang and danced in a single movement; he learned to do it too, without moving a muscle in his face, or mouth, or throat.

He, the boy, realized just then that the hard clay of the volcano was suddenly a road, a flat tongue of earth, fine gravel for tires, clean and well lit by streetlights. At the hour when traffic came to a standstill, the old mother began to sing. Then came the rain, mud again, and out of the mud emerged shapes that hopped off toward the trees; frogs, hundreds of them, heading for his tree, before the wheels of the truck of the company arrived with the light of day.

He, tired, could hear the old mother:

"You can do what my mother and my mother's mother, and her mother's mother, and their mothers and fathers, and the eldest mothers and fathers, and the mothers of the eldest mothers and fathers did, but this place where they did it will no longer be here.

"That doesn't mean you cannot climb into the tree, pursue the blood of birds, or leap from the highest boughs onto the volcano, even if they try to make you believe that it's just a mound of gravel, that the water belongs to a man, and that you're nothing more than the wheelchair where you read, that supports and holds you upright, and the glass screen that turns your blinking eyes into words that can't keep a secret.

"The Band is where your Band has ended up."

I, on the other hand, sleep and make corrections without closing my eyes.

9.
CORRECTION

The choreography needs a stage. Back then, the other had just turned fourteen. His mother was insistently calling to him from another room in the hotel suite, exclaiming with feigned enthusiasm that he should come, that the waves out in the cold sea had turned back into slugs, enormous and black, rushing in and washing over the coast, swallowing the locals. The other was muttering swear words he learned watching movies.

Late that night, he woke up with a melody in his head, two bass lines in eighth and whole notes, that made him grab his keyboard, write down the notes, and repeatedly subject them to that automatic arpeggio. The ambassador, apoplectic, opened the door, walked over to the bed, and ripped the keyboard from his hands, asking in his always-monotone voice if he wasn't ashamed for having woken his mother, who probably wouldn't fall back asleep for the rest of the night. The other stayed in the dark, looking out the window, rabid, spitting at the faint silhouette of a face that took shape against the darkness and the rain, imagining it was the figure of the ambassador. But it was just his own reflection, and that made him so angry that he decided he was going to use the new underwear his mother had left him in the dresser drawer to wipe the mess of spit off the window. But he didn't do it. He just opened the window and stood there for a while, looking out at the sea, and then it occurred to him that the waves did, in effect, look like slugs, absorbing the rain and rising, with impunity, to swallow anyone who might venture out along the seashore. It upset him that the same thing had occurred to his mother hours earlier—how unoriginal. Around eight in the morning, the ambassador interrupted his reverie, placing his hands on his shoulders as he spoke to him. The other couldn't hear him and just watched his mouth moving, because the volume was turned all the way up on his headphones. He started laughing. His father tore off his headphones with a quick swipe. Listen up: he had thirty minutes to shower, shave, and get dressed. His suit was on the table. In thirty minutes, he repeated, the driver would come by to collect him and take him to the ceremony at the church. He and his mother had to leave earlier. The ambassador was a close friend of the general.

The other shut himself in the bathroom until he heard his parents leave with a slam of the door, after having stood in the doorway for more than five minutes, giving him instructions. He found an umbrella, took the key to the suite, walked down the hallway, got in the elevator, and went down to the hotel's first floor. He ordered an espresso at the bar and sat down in a leather armchair in the corner, settling in to watch the rain fall out on the water, while smoking a fat cigar he'd found in a suitcase. Behind the bar, a woman and two waiters were looking at each other, smiling, whatever words they spoke were inaudible. In the middle of the restaurant, a foreigner told his local companion that no, that nothing and nobody could get him to discuss his black hair in an interview, those grays had cost him too much grief decades back. Then, for long minutes, they ate clams in silence, a silence broken only to praise the quality of whatever wine they were drinking.

As he looked out the window and noticed with unease that the waves had already taken the sidewalk across the street, as a distant echo asked what color was the sea, the other distinctly heard in his head the four bass lines that he'd transformed into a base rhythm on his keyboard, and to which he now added a pipe organ, a xylophone, and strumming, plus four gospel singers for the chorus, and the deep melody of a doom-metal guitar. And he began to hear certain words, lyrics that fifteen years later would be the opening lines on The Band's first album; he began to hear the lyrics, yes, but not the voice that sang them. How was that possible? he was asking himself when, at the other table, the tourists interrupted his thoughts with cries for more wine, more clams, another ashtray.

It was becoming hard to tell if outside it was pouring rain or if the fog was just very dense, and then, arbitrarily, the light of a streetlamp blinked into existence. The other was able to make out a taxi pulling up along the curb and a girl getting out of it. Her arms barely managing to hold onto a rain-soaked stuffed animal of absurd dimensions. The other got to his feet, grabbed an umbrella, and ran out between the tables, down the hallway, through the hotel lobby, across the sidewalk and street, between the cars, behind the taxi. In the downpour and honking horns he was unable to find her. She had probably gone into one of the buildings along the avenue; he gave up. Just as he was bringing his eyes back down from the buildings, a man in athletic attire ran right into him. They brushed themselves off. Both swallowed a quick apology, exchanged nods. Then the man snatched the umbrella out of his hand and took off running, just as a wave rolled in and broke over the other.

The chorcography needs a libretto. He is not the other. She comes now with a cup of tea and strokes my hair in the same way that she takes a glass of wine and wraps her arms around the other in bed.

I, on the other hand, can write a line of jacket copy for this autobiographical fiction that keeps no secrets, if morning comes in through the window, alights on my face, and dazzles me like the blind chicken that flaps around far away from the bonfire and turns to stone when caught in the headlights of a truck traveling down a dirt road in the night:

"This book isn't a story of excesses, betrayals, business negotiations, abandonments, alliances, accidents, and reunions.

"The Band doesn't begin when its members meet, but when each of them recognizes for the first time that they are the instrument of whoever is playing."

I am he. Not the other. My brother didn't die when I stabbed him, the prison didn't begin when I turned myself in, covered in blood, at the port's third precinct. The volcano won't turn into a hill even if a millennium of commerce consumes its slopes. The old mother lets them go to the city with the boys but not the girls; one night, when they got back, the chickens were hanging bloodless, and in the morning they found the kawellu gutted atop the gravel heap. In the end, the paper company comes and cuts down his tree along with millions of others; his tree, but not his brother's tree, which adorns our office garden to this day.

He, the star, bought that company and so many others: accordingly, I no longer have a hand resting on the bark of a tree, just my eyelashes pressing against the surface of a glass screen. In that city where he and his brother grew up, nothing grew. They ran, raging through the streets until one of them glimpsed the sea for the first time, until one of them touched snow for the first time, until one of them breathed in the jungle air for the first time. So his brother had to die too.

I, on the other hand, let myself be sliced up repeatedly by the saw of electricity on stages in many different places that, nevertheless, were identical: lights on my face, on the other's hands, on her torso, on the groins of the two bassists, on the feet of the masses come to dance with our vapor, our projections.

I am he, no longer with any ability to turn my back on the smoke or the screen.

He, the boy, stopped in front of the tongue of earth, where trucks were still passing by loaded with security guards, helmets, and machine guns, searching for the old mother. He stood at the edge of the stage. Hands pressed against the nape of his neck, he sustained a scream that didn't require him to move a single facial muscle and that, at the same time, contorted those of the people who heard it. Because his tree was about to fall. I, paralyzed, correct this autobiography:

"She is as important as the other, as the two bassists, as the masses called audience, because she's blinded, like the old mother who disappears beyond the hills, in the direction of the volcano."

The Band is also I. It is my land even if I can no longer be there; a land, mine, made not of land, or metal, or glass.

8.
CORRECTION

The choreography needs a libretto: Cueros was officially started in the summer of 1986, on a patio in the Santiago neighborhood of La Florida by a set of twins, children of a linotype operator and a nurse who worked at José Joaquín Aguirre hospital. Those were the days of Latin rock playing on the radio, but instead of hits by Upa!, Soda Stereo, GIT, the twins listened to tapes that a friend of their father, living in exile in Stockholm, sent to them, with songs by bands like the Chameleons, Television, and the Cocteau Twins.

It was around that time, in high school, that his brother met his future wife, Sara, the sister of a popular performance artist, who a decade later became a set designer for nationally syndicated TV shows. Before long, the twins were regulars at Garage Matucana, where they heard the Electrodomésticos, Viena, and La banda del pequeño vicio play over and over. The twins made their first record on their home stereo: he played guitar and sang lead vocals; his brother played bass, sang vocal harmonies, and used the drum-machine feature on a toy keyboard that belonged to Sara's little sister to create the beat. Cueros played Garage Matucana three times, with guest performances featuring Sara on recorder and Igor Rodríguez—of Aparato Raro—on synthesizer. Two songs they composed

25

during that period were recorded professionally and included on the compilation, released by the Alerce label, *Nuevo rock nacional, volumen 4*.

Alerce signed them on to record a full-length album. In October of 1987, *La pieza de Sara* was distributed in two popular record stores and sold an unexpected 330 copies, with zero promotional support beyond word of mouth. A manager, whose name is unknown, offers to represent them. Already distancing themselves from Garage Matucana, in the summer of 1988, the twins bring in Arturo Soto on drums and the Argentine Clemente Ferlosio on keyboards, who play multiple shows with them in discotecas up and down the central coast, culminating at the second annual Festival Free in Bellavista, where they share the stage with Aterrizaje Forzoso, Lambda, and— the headliner—Los Prisioneros.

An Argentine tour at the end of the year coincides with the release of the Cueros second single, *En el techo*, onto the Buenos Aires airwaves. The magazine *Cerdos y peces* put it on their Song of the Month list. They toured the provinces on the other side of the Andes for four months and even crossed another border to do a show at a bar in Foz de Iguaçu. In the subsequent months, Arturo Soto leaves the band and the vocalist meets Dudú Branca, a fusion percussionist, playing with John McLaughin at the time, in Brasilia, and his brother marries Sara and takes a job as a producer for Sony Music Argentina.

In April 1991, Cueros release the EP, *La escalera de J*, on Alerce, whose blank green cover—a nod to the vocalist's recent conversion to Rastafarianism—was replaced at the last minute by a photograph of Copacabana in the summer. None of the Cueros albums, or those of the subsequent Sismos and Jim Nace, included any information beyond the production credits; of the twins, there only exists one tiny monochrome portrait that experts picked out in the collage depicting the recent electronic compilation of Gymnastics's greatest hits. A second EP, from July of 1991, *Las fotos reveladas*, would be Cueros' final record. On August 16th, they sign on with EMI for two albums and record a live performance of the single "Labiales y velas" for the TV show *Undercriollo*, on UCV-TV. Because of the variety of rhythmic and melodic references in their songs—60s British psychedelia, gringo Gospel, and New Wave, but also Jamaican rhythms, Peruvian Chicha, Old School East Coast Hip Hop, Brazilian tropicalia, the sunshine pop of the Beach Boys, Pehuenche ceremonial music, industrial postpunk, ambient, the anti-cuecas of Violeta Parra, and the jazz of Sun Ra—which, according to Argentine music critics, baffled the public, Cueros would have no doubt achieved a musical synthesis that would've gone on to animate the listless pop produced in the Southern Cone in the following decades, if it hadn't been for that fatal August night in 1991, when the vocalist stabbed his twin brother.

The choreography needs simultaneity. I close my eyes and repeat this con-
tinuously, for I have neither larynx, nor lips, nor palate with which to sing
a word that remains hidden.

    He, in his prison, realized that the best way to shave, to look himself
in the eyes, to pluck hairs, and to check for food in his teeth wasn't with a
mirror, which were prohibited; a guard had been stabbed and a tunnel dug
with their sharp, broken points. He, in his prison, figured out that he could
see his reflection in the window.

    I, on the other hand, blink and am not tired. I move my pupil, there's no
longer a ngürütrewa *to follow with my eyes up the mountainside, while*
awaiting the right moment to steal the kawellu *and bring it to the old*
mother on a rope, furious, kicking, just like her, to remove the hair from
its belly, to hear it whinny with pride, to let it rest its muzzle against my
leg instead of my neck.

    He, in his prison, was looking out the window at the hills. He guessed
that the sun danced blue on those slopes because, in front of them, was a
great body of water, because the ocean was right there. So the punishment
was that he understood when people spoke to him of the sea, that he was
even allowed to go to the window and stare out at its reflection, but that
none of the windows had a view of the coast. He'd never seen the sea; he

told the four men who came to rape him the place at the window was his
and he wasn't going to give it up.

I, on the other hand, sit in front of a window that's not transparent. A
piece of glass that corrects me if I don't dilate my pupil, opening new windows where neither hills nor what's beyond the hills appears when I blink
three times in a row; that alerts me when I need eye drops by reflecting a
vein in my eyeball. She comes in and I see in the blankness of the screen
how she kisses me, how she puts her hand on the nape of my neck, how in
her language she sings to me.

I, on the other hand, erase what remains in the window.

He, in his prison, was defending his place by the windows, because
he had seen her out walking, as an adolescent girl, across one of the hills.
For a month, she entered through the same door. She appeared on the same
upper-story balcony, leaned against the railing, and stayed there, looking
back at him; behind her, on the back wall in the room she rented, he could
also make out a poster with the other's face and the name of another band.

He, in his prison, was defending his place by the windows where she
once appeared and kicked out the glass panes in which his brother saw
him again.

I, on the other hand, sit in front of this blank screen. I let what my
eyelids write be corrected on a soft, pleasing, polished surface—neither tree
bark nor quicksilver nor glass:

"I am he. The Band begins where the couple formed by me and the old
mother, me and my brother, she and the other ends. The Band ends where
the couple begins."

I correct and let myself be corrected.

He, in his prison, writes on the fogged glass with his finger before the
guards come, before four of them grab him for having broken the window.
I am he and I blink incessantly until my eyes swell shut.

8.
CORRECTION

The choreography needs simultaneity. On the first flight, she and he never once let go of each other's hand, not even when the producer handed her a glass of *piñón* juice and he, with his bare foot, tickled her to make her drop it. They didn't let go four hours later either, when, night already falling, they got up and locked themselves in the bathroom while the bassists spouted dirty jokes and the other, pretending to be asleep, turned up the volume of the most recent album that the company had uploaded onto his device. The general mood was quite different a hundred and forty-four hours later, when the other, in suit and tie, and he, in pajamas, connected from their separate rooms, finished mixing the record's final track and, coming together in front of their respective cameras, each gave their consent; then they opened the recording studio's hermetically sealed doors and the remaining three members of The Band quickly escaped into the parks that ran parallel the banks of the city's canals.

She unbuttoned her black jacket's bottom button and walked. She paused on a bridge whose name she couldn't pronounce, rested her hands on the parapet, and was surprised by how cold the bricks were. The wind whipped her long hair, she placed a hand over her stomach, clouds entered her field of vision, birds flew by in the distance, a warm wind picked up just as the air began to tremble with the tolling bells of the church behind her. For a moment, she wasn't his toy, as the other had called her the night before, drunk, when he offered her a zillionth pill, after, once again, declaring his love for her. She realized that whose six days spent recording their second record had been another farce. To be a vocalist you have to lie, the other told her more than once, late at night, coming back from some concert, driving the pickup or riding the subway. When he knew she was paying attention, he added: you're so pretty. She bit her tongue, squinted her eyes, and watched the people out the window; every now and then she saw the vocalist's stride, one of his extravagant hairdos, in someone else, someone shouting or someone doubled over on the ground, playing the harmonica outside one of the empire's philanthropic institutions. Then, in a low voice she'd tell him, in her language: don't tell me I'm pretty. There, as the bells of some church rang out, she forgot the fifty-three times the vocalist made her repeat the opening line of the third song, his sharp tone, the time his bony fist struck the transparent panel—with such force that the surface undulated like a sheet—because she'd lost the beat at the intro to the final suite. He doesn't love himself, only his predecessors, the voice of the other repeated in her head, and the sun in the city was suddenly hidden, so the blue of the canals and the red of the bricks became steely surfaces. But if the vocalist was going to modify her beats in the studio anyway, why was she even in The Band?

She unbuttoned the second button, stuck her hands in her pockets, and found a mushroom chocolate. She tossed three pieces into her mouth. A nun sat down beside her and patted her thigh and told her that love is all one, though its forms vary, like how on a good night, the nebulas and constellations are faintly reflected in the canal. She laughed and the nun got to her feet, offended. That night, she noticed the wind had stopped, then the streets stretched out in all directions. Now her skin was the grass in the park where she lay down, the lights that she could truly touch with just her gaze from on the ground. She'd lost one of her jacket buttons, she found it in her mouth. He wasn't he. She was crying and when the bassists found her, all she could do was babble.

Two hours later she accepted a beer in the club and drinking it she felt better. She was recovering a particular sensation from when she was just a few years old in the suburbs, when her parents were celebrating some anniversary with distant relatives; she, only a few years old, moved between their legs, and a rhythm played that took hold of her, hands made of music took her by the waist and she danced atop a table and no one cared that plates and glasses crashed to the floor. The first cardiac, guttural, muffled bars of two basses and a drum machine shook the club, she chugged her beer and joined the euphoric mass on the dance floor. Through her own cries, she recognized a voice speaking to her: the other was trying to dance beside her. They laughed. She knew that beat that had pulled her onto the dance floor, that voice that compelled all those people to dance, was the third song on their album. When a group of dancing kids surrounded them, grinding their pelvises against them, she understood that they'd worked only a short time and yet they'd earn a great deal of money, that for that reason The Band wouldn't last, that they'd all end up living somewhere far away.

The choreography needs counterpoint. When I close my eyes, I can occupy certain names from the innumerable languages I was recorded in, but when I open them I'm unable to transcribe, blinking onto the screen, a single one of their sounds, if she doesn't come in with the first light of the rising sun to cleanse my palette with her freshly brushed teeth.

He, the boy, ran to the mouth of the river where nobody went for fear of the pancora *and the* cuero *to practice long concatenations of sounds that competed with the tireless voices of the water gurgling off every stone, the call of the* piurrín *to the departing sun, the whirr of the dragonfly, the buzz of the bumblebee, the word that could only be sung by the old mother up in her tree.*

He, running through the neighborhood with his brother, scratched long concatenations of sounds across the walls of the factories in colors never before seen, not even when the fog obscured the dawn on the other side of the volcano; and yet, a few hours later, the names turned gray, absorbed by the city, the filth of its air, the hardened clay of its pavement. Then his brother gave him a charley horse and forced him to sing with his muscles seizing, as they scrawled the string of incomprehensible signs, waiting to fire their slingshots at the eyes of the security guards who would arrive with sirens and flashlights.

I open just one eye, so the screen cannot correct me: the autobiography of The Band is a story of screams and threats, but not one shot was ever fired.

He, the singer, stopped a concert in a theater of marionettes, kings, millionaires, executives, and fraudsters when the bouncers beat a fan who tried to get up on the stage. He, the star, spit on the feet of the producers who teased him, asking why he went home so early at night, wasn't he Hispanic. I am he. I've never prayed, but I did take the hands of the fan, of the old mother, of the boys, of the bassists, of she and the other, drunk in bed, on the warm beach, we were three when the sun came up and she said in her island language that somebody had stolen our clothes, in a low voice she proposed that we go find leaves in the bushes and instead we found a rabbit that had escaped from its wachi.

She calls to me with the word that I say as I close my eyes.

He, wanting to strike her, wept for the first time in her presence, looking out at the sea.

He, the singer, opened his hands and opened his arms and opened his chest and opened his stomach and opened his groin and opened his legs and opened his feet before opening his lips.

He, in prison, got up before the sun in order to recite his litany in secret, but more than once four men emerged from some confusion on the cellblock and found him there, eyes closed, facing the fog on the window.

He, in prison, succeeded in turning inward and forming a point at the exhalation of the last sound, mouth almost shut where the limbs lashed his palate, as a kick from one of the four men broke his nose. They didn't know that they were helping him amplify that mouthless whistle, that the blood would be a thread that would take him to exalted places, though what they saw was him spasming on the floor, glass embedded in his scalp, fingers spread, toes bent.

He, in her arms, asked her not to wake him every time he opened his mouth screamlessly in his sleep. She knows that he sleeps little, that he closes his eyelids to locate the sound of a concatenation of names capable of quieting the whispers that gave him that swagger while crossing stages in different lands of colors he and his twin had never seen, neither through fog nor smoke. She knows she can speak for him, though she does so in the language of the island and the language of the peninsula, in the language of the rabbits and the language of the kawellus, *in the whisper of screens and in the whisper of books. She takes his hands and doesn't say she finds them cold, runs her nails lightly across the nape of his neck and licks his eyelashes; then she returns to the bed and lets the other wrap his arms around her.*

I, on the other hand, sit in front of the impeccable surface with eyelids steadily searching for the right word that isn't autobiography.

7.
CORRECTION

The choreography needs counterpoint. Sitting on a bench in the plaza, the other heard how the voices swelled inside the cathedral as sporadic drops gave way to rain. He opened his eyes and got ready to stand, to make his way through the crowd of shaved- and dreadlock-headed kids, covered in tattoos, who were beginning to shout insults at the riot police, obtained by the widow thanks to her friendship with the mayor.

Before entering the funeral, the other reflexively rolled up the sleeves of his white shirt. The bishop's litanies made him drowsy and there, amid votive candles, eulogies, and kerchiefs dabbing eyes and noses of the venerable elderly, senators, and diplomats— relatives no doubt of the widow and not of her husband, the mentor—the other was able to fall deeply asleep for the first time in ten days, and thereby ignore the obvious swelling in his phalanges and tendons, resulting from the demanding schedule of rehearsals he'd been submitted to in recent days. On his deathbed, the mentor had provided him with instructions for how each of the twelve songs should be played, while struggling to hold up the weight of the tube organ and transistor sequencer, of the eight-track recorder and analog mixer, running the risk the equipment would tangle with the tube that had just fed him against his will, hanging on until the final chord of The Band Project's thirtieth record was recorded.

The other heard the suite that would close that final album like a litany repeated by the thirty voices that crescendoed in the cathedral as the bishop bade farewell to the mentor, he said, to his time on this earth. Then the mentor was alive again, though dying, in his bed, while the other, sitting at his side, disguised the beeping of the monitors with an improvisation, starting out with an acoustic-guitar andante, because he knew that the mentor—who ate only vegetables and didn't drink alcohol, who had never ingested pills or worked with other musicians until the other, when he was seventeen years old, was hired as his cook and managed to gain his trust as a guitarist; who practiced every morning, sequestered himself every afternoon, and renounced sex every night—didn't listen to anything but Bach, Fela Kuti, and Felt. The blue skin of the mentor faded, fog filled the dream but not the image of those feverish eyes that the other saw cloud over when the mentor learned from the mouths of his doctors that he wouldn't be able to complete his work on The Band Project, that he wouldn't last long enough to finish recording the thirteen songs of the thirtieth and last album that was to close the cycle with the music of a possible biology behind the metaphysical practice; there was satisfaction in those eyes, because at last the pains of his illness would come to an end.

"In his Presence," the bishop repeated.

Those words still hung in the other's somnolent ears, in the cathedral, when he started awake, discovering a thread of drool seeping, almost imperceptibly, out of his mouth. God, he thought in his island language, at what point did it occur to me to roll up my shirtsleeves in this cold? Then—as an antique organ marked the footsteps of the widow's relatives, walking down the aisle, bearing the casket of the man whose Band Project had topped the charts three times with its first album, as late-arriving fans watched the procession with perplexity from the seats in back of the cathedral, and as the reporters raised their cameras above the crowd—the other understood the origin of the reflex that had made him roll up his shirtsleeves before entering the funeral; he'd forgotten about how, when the ambassador told him over the phone that his mother had left to go live in the mountains with a guerrilla missionary, he was washing the dishes, holding the phone between shoulder and ear, so he had rolled up the sleeves of his shirt. The cold of the water shot up his arms along with the certainty that he'd never see her again.

The police had been deployed at the door to the cathedral and were pushing back the shaved- and dreadlock-headed kids, protesting the imminent burial of the mentor in a Catholic cemetery. For them, it was an affront to the Reichian Marxism he declaimed on the fifth installment of The Band Project, the double album with the sunflower cover, and they shouted slogans opposing the new contract, announced that morning by the widow in a TV interview, to rerelease his discography. From a corner on the stairs, behind the police cordon, over the sirens, through the entreaties of an ecclesiastical authority, above the cameras, and amid the growing mass of onlookers who weren't approaching from the plaza, the other focused his attention on one heavyset kid, spouting off in yet another language. It was the vocalist. He remembered the impotent rage in the eyes of the mentor when he failed to play a syncopated rhythm on his guitar. He hurried toward the hearse, not caring anymore that the widow, the multinational record label, the military police, the shaved heads, the fan club, and the churches opposed it: he had decided to finish the last Band Project album on his own. That very night, he would record and mix the thirteen songs he'd glimpsed in his dream, the thirteen structures, the thirteen rhythms, the thirteen arrangements, the thirteen titles, the thirteen lyrics, and his own thirteen counterpoints that had come to him just then, amid all that mediocrity, as if they were those of the mentor, a second before a rock, flying through the air, struck him in the temple.

The choreography needs accumulation. I, on the other hand, am paralyzed in front of an immaculate, unblemished, un-cracked, unscratched screen.

He, the singer, kept closing his eyes and heightening the sensation in his skin whenever the voice rose from his stomach; prickling, he received the uploads from The Band, he stopped hearing the voice when, not even looking at each other, she and the other and the two bassists and the hired keyboardist stopped repeating their parts and began to elaborate separate variations that, in his prison, made him think of the movement of roots when the sun emerges.

"No, no one leaf is the same as the next," the old mother would say if he got too close to the tree.

"Every time the sun shines, the stem ages, grows, or shrivels, whatever's left evaporates and turns into rain."

Just then, the way opened up and he, the singer, raised his voice so that she and the other and the two bassists and the hired keyboardist could, together, take what came from his hands somewhere far away. I, on the other hand, am sustained just by taking deep breaths and blinking. I have no way to stretch my clothes so my skin can breathe and to find, with The Band, a beat for which hundreds of people had put the little food they had on our plates, where our bare feet rested and, from there inside, would *shoot off in every direction, little by little, sighing in some hidden corner, movement, amassing.*

I am he, I saved up enough to get a wheelchair. And he, the singer, let himself fall into the masses that were waiting to break apart only to come back together when nobody asked for it, that had decided to grip the feet of The Band in their fists. The trunk whispered to him that neither the rain nor the snow nor the chainsaw would make him fall out of the tree he was climbing; the whisper was the deepest scream of that thing that has no name and never will, for it hasn't been opened or shut, in the blink of an eye, masses accumulating, telling the story of The Band. Hearing his scream, they decided to dance, to let themselves be moved by a different beat, whisper, and vibration, coming from their own mouths. A single mass rushed to the center of the field, broke apart, crashed to the ground in the stadium, but nobody, except for the security guards, stepped on anyone.

The Band down in front of the stage is I.

She and the other and those others and the others am I: a tree that was pure root, a blue stain in a space resembling a wasteland, a lake seeping through stone opened by flameless fire, red water frozen for whoever might need to drink it, a hand in the night inside her mouth and the other's mouth. He, the singer, lying there, vapor roiling across the floor, suddenly understood the word that had come to him from out the dancing masses; neither the name of his twin nor that of the other nor that of the old mother, not the stone he'd found in the jungle when aging made him shed his insect-bite-ridden skin: it was his own name in a language he couldn't pronounce.

I, on the other hand, wait for her to come and touch me late in the night, just before the engines start sounding in the streets. These eyelids try to push her away and, when I shut first one and then the other and blink them immediately back open, the screen assumes I am erasing every character in the autobiography until, exhausted, both lids fall shut and all corrections are unmade.

7.
CORRECTION

The choreography needs accumulation. The baroque organist and composer, Johann Sebastian Bach, is considered the most influential musician in the history of Western music, not just because of the meticulous virtuosity of his pieces, but because of the scope of his compositions. Lawrence Hayward, front man and soul of the band Felt, who doesn't appear in any musicological index of the twentieth century, moved from postpunk garage to lounge jazz and ambient, with stops along the way in new wave and folk, across a limited selection of songs. These two artists, of vastly dissimilar projects, converged unexpectedly in harmonies of The Band Project in the 80s and 90s. Inspired by the project of his friend and rival, Lawrence, the mentor planned a musical project that, straddling the line between Felt's rhythmicity and Bach's aspiration to infinity, spanning twelve years and twelve albums, would explore the twelve connections that, for him, constituted the chain of life, unfazed by successive accusations of forgetting where he came from, of anthroposophism, of art for art's sake, of gnosis, and of sexual conservatism that would belatedly mark the reception of his albums. Illness forced him to prolong the completion of his work from twelve to thirteen years, a number charged with interpretations, though entirely lacking the symmetry he was seeking.

In its first five years, The Band Project seemed like it was going to reach a wide audience; its first three albums shot up the sales charts and the imperial media took great pleasure in making irrelevant comparisons between Band Project shows and those of progressive rockers who in decades past raked in millions playing sold-out stadiums. As the years went by, the fundamental tension the mentor maintained between rawness and artifice became more relevant in popular music; the catchy synthesizer riffs and the guitar atmospheres clashed with the explosion, the bass drum, and the scream, in such a way that the mentor became a musician only invited to perform by anti-imperial conservation institutions. The Band Project's later albums were released on record labels of the worker's collective; there were no more shows or sales, the mentor shut himself away in his studio and not a single reporter had any interest in finding out why. His death would change all of that. The year before, out of nowhere, there had been a rash of famous dance bands claiming him explicitly as musical model, and that pretense of authenticity would establish the supreme value of a new imitative aesthetic. Continental clubs incessantly played new danceable electronica versions of some of The Band Project's anthems and pop music radio stations even played some singles from The Band's second album, itself an homage to and, at the same time, a break from The Band Project. The fact that those albums are now available again is due in large part to the interest of fans who demand more and more of The Band's material and who unconsciously see in that experimental voice that leads the choral and percussive masses a prefiguration of their own vocalist, who nevertheless, unlike the guitarist, never knew the mentor. "We musicians envy the class struggle, for none of you will ever listen to us the way you listen to your political leaders," the vocalist said ironically in front of the crowd of kids who gathered in that southern desert valley for the release of The Band's last album. Only a few people recognized those words, the words with which the mentor brought to an end his final interview, when, the day before his death, he announced that his last album would be left unfinished: "We musicians envy the sacred, because of the way people who believe in the existence of some intangible thing listen."

The choreography needs displacement. I am he and he is the other, and the other insists that she come back to bed, instead of repeatedly stretching her groin, so the muscles send blood to the tendons in her foot.

With blood he, the boy, and the old mother were weaving string, like pancora rippling the surface of the water on the river. Following the marks the rain left on the fields, the old mother went to the place where she kept her stones, everyone's stones, and all the other stones we could throw at the security guards of the paper mill.

He, recording, realized that it wasn't his voice that hung in the air, but an echo. His problem, he'd tell the other in the middle of a heated discussion, when she and the two bassists had gone out to walk along the canals of that vacationing city, was that they were shut inside a glass box where their voices reverberated back at them, instead of finding a way to be exalted, exposed, released like insects gnawing their way deep into underground aquifers to protect themselves, to be knotted to the sticks that weiraos and coypus gathered to avoid the currents; the voice had to get lost so that someone else could discover the name of the person who lets it go when they hear it.

He, recording, didn't expect anyone to understand his poorly translated words. So they shook hands when the other unexpectedly took out his keys,

*a bottle, hoisted a recording device onto his shoulder, and asked that he go
with him. He rented a boat, pushed it out from the shore where the water
made their legs glow, and said: now sing.*

*I, on the other hand, can only come face to face with the narrowing of
these eyes in the homogenous, hard, and unbreakable surface where the
blinking of my eyes writes and erases. The autobiography of The Band,
underlined with the lowering of a brow, is neither the story of the other
nor of her enlightenment, nor a character study starring the vocalist, no,
it is the barbed wire, the streams, the tracks, the signs, and the pathways
that divide these lands as they connect them. The mass of flesh, weaving
together muscle, skin, tendon, vein, lymph, nameless matter, nerve, and
bone doesn't constitute a specific organ: it is our body.*

*He, the boy, squinted his eyes but couldn't shut them when, coming
down from the high boughs, he saw some unfamiliar birds pecking at the
fingernails of the old mother, who had been tossed out of a truck belonging
to the company that owned all the paper mills onto a pile of burnt leaves,
between his and his twin brother's trees.*

*He, singing, remembered that the old mother's footsteps had to encom-
pass not just the hill where they were walking but the river they were
skirting and the volcano where they were heading, not just the* kawellu
that showed him the way, but also the witranalwe *clutching the eggs in
its talons, making him want to turn back, the* pillanes *and the imps, the
insomniacs and the snorers. He, in his prison, was unable to privilege in
his memory the old mother's remains over the way she moved when she
danced and sang, for to do so would be to forget that his own unknown
name included her name, the name of the chicken and the goats, of the old
mother's mother's mother, and of that place that is in all places.*

*"To each their own tree," the percussionist would say in her island
language when it dawned on her that he, tired, had brought her to live on
lands he'd bought for her.*

"For a tree isn't a tree, it's a vertical forest, a conjuring of boughs, insects, birds, fungi, larvae, vapors, and other creatures that don't want to be seen and we don't want to see."

He, tired, sat down in his chair and never got up again.

I am he. He grew old because she, though she wouldn't know how to say the name to him, had heard it. I, in hers and in all places, keep on blinking: what I previously set out before me to pulsate in the sun only appears now if I shut my eyes.

7.
CORRECTION

The choreography needs displacement. She kissed him. For a long time. Then she was alone, inside a small room full of her cousin's doll collection. Through the door, she'd heard somebody say her father's funeral would take place that very night, but as a three or four year old, she could never resist the drowsiness that came over her, without fail, as soon as the sun went down, her eyelids grew heavy and she fell asleep. So she got into the bed; it was a white-lacquered wooden bunk bed whose mattresses came together to form a T. She coughed. She shivered with chills under the covers. She stretched a little and found a pile of cushions atop her legs. They're so hard, she said to herself, getting up to remove them. And it was then she discovered her father's corpse, wrapped in the sheets at her feet.

She woke up from the fright. It was ten in the morning; the cool breeze of springtime in the old empire's capital came in through the window accompanied by the song of a bird and occasional honks from out in the street. Beside her, the bed was empty; the pillows on the floor. The vocalist had meticulously wrapped the percussion-ist's legs in blankets and down comforters, so she had to struggle to stand up. He'd also built a sort of tower with the hotel cushions on top of her feet. Where had he gone, she wondered, and scanned with her eyes for the underwear, the wrinkled pants, and the metal belt he'd thrown in a corner last night, after skillfully removing them, the glasses and the pills he'd deposited on the nightstand while she showered. In vain. She didn't remember what time he'd left the room, all she could summon was the terror of having touched a dead body, her father's body, in her dream, and a vague melody that at times was a faint hum. Was her family alive? She was still rehearsing in her mind the long-distance international and national codes for her home city when the ringing of the telephone on the nightstand made her jump out of bed.

Five hours later, she was waiting, in the backseat of a taxi, for a guard to return her documents and open the forbidding gate of the widow's residence. On the way, she had amused herself looking at the shapes of the clouds that appeared in the northern sky. Every time she called the vocalist, she got a message saying his phone was no longer in service. Twice she was tempted to call the other to ask him if he had seen the vocalist, both times she settled for finding the back of a horse in the nimbuses, the legs of a spider, the silhouette of a cat resembling the Siamese her little cousin adored. The butler let her into the residence. She waited in a hall adorned with two hanging chandeliers, sitting on the edge of a divan, facing two huge oil paintings. It was just how she imagined the inside of an old-empire castle. She smiled not out of happiness, but because she was imagining the bitter pantomime the other would do as soon he entered that place; he would look around and allege that these people all think everything from the past should be a museum, just so she could retort that in that case he should propose a remodel and put an illuminated glass pyramid in the center of it. What do you know, the other would fire back, that you didn't read in some tourist guidebook. During the half hour she spent waiting for the widow, as the staff refilled her cup, she forced herself to maintain these internal dialogues to keep from thinking about the keys: there was a grand piano glowing in the middle of the hall. The top was open. After ten minutes, she couldn't help but stare from the divan at the whiteness of the keys, while fingering from memory and from afar, eighth note by eighth note, a polonaise that her father frequently played on their piano, at home, in the summer.

The widow interrupted her reverie when she entered the hall, trailed by a assistant. They went over the dates of The Band's tour through the ruins of the cities; they discussed the weather and the advantages of traversing the old empire in taxi. They were silent. She tasted the chamomile tea they had brought her to ameliorate the effect of successive coffees, she felt like there was a viscous paste on her tongue.

"Do you like my hall?" asked the widow.

She nodded.

"And the piano?"

She shrugged.

"Drums are my thing."

She was lying. Then the widow stood up and ceremoniously closed the wide doors.

"You know," she said, after sitting back down, "I feel like I can trust you. It's been a long time since I felt that way."

Then she looked cheekily at her assistant, who exhaled audibly.

"A long time, to tell the truth. Every time I've met with musicians in my various homes, for thirty years, none of them has ever been able to resist sitting down at the piano and playing some of their dreck while I make them wait. You're the first one who has shown any respect."

The widow took off her glasses and began to adjust her hair. Is it possible this woman reminds me of my cousin? the percussionist thought to herself. The widow looked at her as if she were expecting a specific response from her. She got to her feet again, walked to a cabinet with double doors. She opened it, removing a bottle and two glasses.

"That's why I want to propose that we do a different sort of business," she said.

The choreography needs its place, there, where he could walk without fear, without laughter, without fantasy, without pride, without property, without subterfuge, and without expectation, across the ground from where the old mother always leapt into the tree, from where the men walking in the street weren't reflected as their twins in the glass of the buildings, from where each person moved in a way distinct from him, singing, and, at the same time, they were all part of the same mass; in the end, a space where he couldn't identify himself, because it was neither country nor city, neither prison nor sea, neither stasis nor dance.

He, the singer, liked that moment when the instruments still resounded, though all the musicians had stopped playing.

He, the singer, let himself be moved by the inertia and the echo of a final syllable that would close his throat in front of the masses. He made no movement, nor did he pause. Pause. She comes with a glass of water and a cotton swab, devotes herself to cleaning the gunk collected in the folds of my eyelids. She insists on the cotton swab and the water, she ignores the cosmetic products that the company I own sends me. Then she gathers the dirty cotton swabs, rewets them and wipes clean the screen here in front of me, while I shut my eyes and pretend to be sleeping, between her legs as her thighs forcefully squeeze me. Finally, she lets me go. I go back to the glow of the glass, she puts the cotton swabs into a bag and drinks down the dirty water in a single swallow.

He, the boy, threw a stone into the water to scare away the cuero. "That was your stone," the old mother said sarcastically behind him.

He, the boy, dove into the river before dawn, shivering with cold, because the pancora wanted to pull him into the holes and because the cuero would tug him down into the depths if his little fingers were unable to find anything solid to hold onto. And yet, as the old mother sang on the shore, the current became crystal clear so he could hear her and in that way find the stone. Then they built a fire that the sun, when it rose, put out with its wind and, when the stone was dry, the old mother added: "That stone doesn't belong to you, none of them do. You need to know this. Neither the cuero, nor the pancora, nor this water are here for your fear, even if justice grows too great and, as I know you will, you end up the owner of all of that which cannot be owned."

He, in his prison, knew the song's place wasn't the silence, wasn't the music, wasn't the noise. The place was a moment.

He, the singer, chose that moment to dive into the masses.

He, tired, built her a greenhouse in the old place where all that was left was his twin's tree. She climbed on top of him and perspired until drops fell from overhead. "An equatorial palm tree and a tundra shrub only intertwine on the narrow earth of the city, never in the country," she murmured in her imperial language, after so many tears and trying to explain herself.

He, tired, went out walking across those lands he would sign and seal over to the company that owns all this paper. He found neither river nor hill, nor the volcano that appeared with the fog.

He, paralyzed, knew his legs belonged to someone else. Someone who took away his groin and his fingers. He would fall and the floor would rise to meet him, with open arms. Before the names came in her scream, in the other's scream, and in the nurses' screams, he brought his hand to his neck: the pancora was ascending toward his mouth.

He, the boy, never understood whether the pancora *went inside and died, if it emerged from another hole, or if it underwent a state change. I, on the other hand, know precisely how to raise just one eyebrow in front of the glowing screen, when there appears a name, a toponymic, a demonym, a year in the autobiography. I am he. The Band cannot be named.*

7.
CORRECTION

The choreography needs its place. Nobody dies of heatstroke in that place. Though if it starts to rain, his friends might be left to float like teabags in boiling water, the tenor gloated with a fixed smile. Beside him, the waiter held out a tray with a dozen glistening glasses; as one of the last remaining aborigines in the region, the Empire paid him and his blood-relatives monthly installments to provide local color at the Protectorate's different official celebrations. The waiter stepped behind the curtain and downed two drinks, looking out the window of the zeppelin to see if the storm was still coming. From overhead the tea plantations gleamed.

Two dark points stained the panorama of those green fields; two figures in motion, running from one side to the other, about to come together when a sound, a call, a slithering animal, or some obstacle—it was impossible to tell from the zeppelin—made the point on the right dart off toward the town. The other kept walking through the southeastern fields of the Protectorate, shaking and swearing, clothes soaked with sweat and his neck sunburnt. He sat down at the base of a tree, he wanted to take off the wool hat he had snatched from her during the argument, before she was lost from sight. That morning, when the security guards brought them down from the zeppelin, as soon as the ATV disappeared back in the direction of the hot air balloon, the other perceived what thereafter he would consider the silence. Then, finally, his head's melody returned, this time a descent of minor notes dropping to the lowest octaves they could thrum; for ten months he'd been hearing nothing but an indistinct noise: tinnitus, they told him; concerts, live shows, recorded interviews, press conferences, board meetings, civil trials, shouted negotiations, sound checks, fireworks, he couldn't distinguish one from the next. Pure feedback. He'd assumed he would never write another harmony when suddenly he saw the landscape of the tea fields. The sight brought him silence, and a song began to compose itself in his mind. That was when she'd leapt on top of him, clawing and biting and spitting, aiming for his throat before taking off running. Sitting at the base of the tree, the other breathed deeply and let the rain wash his face. And it dawned on him that her voice, despite her cries of rage or her sighs, was the one tone that, at the last second, was thrown into relief by the specter of itself. He regretted the moment he'd agreed to climb aboard the hot air balloon the company provided its artists. He did not regret, definitely not, punching the decrepit contemporary video artist who attempted to extinguish his cigarette on the waitress's ass; against all odds, the percussionist had set down her drink and proposed they ditch the gala, run to the fuselage, and find a small hatch that would open onto a biplane, aboard which they would be able to return to the peripheries and join the resistance, like in the songs of yesteryear.

Hours later, the other walked into the nearby town. At a bar, he asked for water, but the woman who was working showed him an empty glass and shook her head with severity. They didn't want his money. He found the percussionist, bathed and calm, on a bench in the square, eyes shut and mouth open, a local man standing in front of her wearing nothing but military pants. The man prodded her palate with a twig. The other walked up uncomprehendingly, reflexively humming the melody that, little by little, was coming back into his head, and sat down on the bench. He took her hand and she turned to him without surprise, without opening her eyes. The man standing in front of her awoke from his trance, lowered the stick, and spoke:

—Death does not want to take you yet, woman. What good fortune.

She covered her mouth with her forearm.

They shook hands, satisfied. As they parted, the man discovered she had managed to slip a bill into the palm of his hand; later he would bury it along with the seed of a new plant.

On their way back to the tea fields, she dodged a kiss the other tried to give her. They ran, savoring the sound of the dry leaves crunching beneath their feet, until they found themselves in a clearing. They looked up at the sky. The rain had stopped. For the next ten days, the afternoon sun would shine bright across the Southeastern Protectorate. The other raised his arms to the zeppelin and began to move.

The choreography needs synchronization. He had practiced every morning ever since, as a kid, he would rise with the first call of the chucao. He, the singer, decided he would devote the first hour of the day to gargling in the motel, where the habit still perplexed him, sun on his face.

He, running through the neighborhood with his brother, knelt down at midday on the church alters. He closed his eyes, opened his legs, relaxed his groin, lowered his zipper, stuck out his chest, leaned his head back to rest the nape of his neck against the wood, spread arms, letting a thread of drool slip from his slack jaw, until the rictus had taken hold of his entire body. Sometimes members of the clergy would take him by the hand, compassionate, until they saw the mess he'd made they'd have to clean. The janitor prodded him out the door with a broomstick and gently let him drop onto the stairs, tossing him a few one-peso coins. A priest, coming in earlier than usual, stood there, staring at him, and then took out his notebook and sketched the position of his body while, at his side, a nun wiped away the smudges his graphite pencil left on the holy cloth.

I, on the other hand, neither perspire nor drool, but force my eyes open until a line of veins forms, running from my temples to the corners of the whites of my eyes, and I proceed to eliminate, across that smooth surface that glows even in the summer, the paragraphs that speak of martyrdom, of sacrifice, of ecstasy, of glory.

He, in his prison, took off his clothes and sat down. He had been pronouncing the same words in all the languages he knew: "detach yourself from yourself with your own arms, remove yourself from yourself." He was stringing together the names the old mother had taught him when, as a boy, she made him climb a hill so that, panting with exhaustion, he would open his mouth and exhale a "young man, macho, warrior," whom later she would bury to the temples, while calling herself "elder, mother, worker, wise woman," and with that throw herself over a precipice releasing an "old man, grandfather, impresario, consultant" along with the constant rain that pattered on the treetops where she landed. He recited them without activating a single facial muscle, without letting his skin move, even when his cellmates woke up fuming in the cool air, furious, drenched in nightmares, and went off on his discipline, on him and the windows, facing the hills where they thought day was breaking.

He, the star, didn't hear the phone calls or the soft raps on the door, the recorded prayers, or silver clinking of the trays laden with honey, cheese, figs, yogurt with cochayuyo, and muday with manjar left for him on the mirrored table, outside all the doors to all his bedrooms and in all the dining rooms where he'd explicitly asked that not a soul enter so he could take off his clothes. As soon as he closed his eyes and tuned in, many languages and registers came to him and there was no need to choose any of them, just allow them to take complete control of his voice, the sound was noise until it coagulated into a rushing mass, expanding with each beat: without end or origin, next to nothing, in all places, and simultaneously crushing him, extruding his eyes from a skin that was fire.

I am he, his are not even chicken bones.

He, paralyzed, found his voice and sang. He achieved it when she kissed his eyelids, when he opened them to her touch and the place was reconstructed before his eyes.

The Band is I, he heard himself say. I, on the other hand, erase.

7.
CORRECTION

The choreography needs synchronization, that of those two bodies, motionless for a moment, bathed in sweat, shuddering and panting. They heard the engine of an airplane beginning to descend toward the airport. He rolled off her, put on his pants, and sat on the convertible's fender, smoking, while she leaned back in the seat and saw how the stars in Central Empire's summer sky were blinking out of sight. Before she drifted off to sleep, the percussionist heard him still intoning his archaic song. For a long second, she maintained focus on the melody the vocalist hummed like a *trompe*. Their argument was far from over.

And she dreamed, in great detail: rising from the tables in that nameless bar, where they had been introduced as The Band for the fourth time, they heard chatter, groans, and heckles that every so often drowned out the volume of their lengthy ballads and the poorly-amplified voice of the vocalist was lost in the thrumming of the two bass guitars, but nobody in the audience seemed to care, probably because the owners had the foresight to bill them as "anti-establishment ambient music" on photocopied posters hung on the door. The vocalist inserted *conchesumares*, *sordosculiaos*, and *sacoweas* into his cries, but nobody was offended, because not a word of his invective-punctuated repertoire was audible over the din. Forty-five minutes later, when she was already snoring in the minivan's backseat, four men in two pickups ambushed them under a yellow streetlight. She poked her head up into the front seat, half asleep, and saw the windshield was covered in spit. There was nobody in the front seats, the doors were open, and she heard the strangers shouting from the street, calling her a whore over and over; she, who had been sleeping the whole time and hadn't even seen the faces of the men insulting her. Amid shouts that brought to mind the free beers offered to everyone in the bar when a spark blew the soundboard and brought the music to a definitive end, the vocalist and the other had taken off after the spitters in the minivan, determined to fight them. Meanwhile, she and the bassist and the other bassist waited for them, sitting in a café along the highway, laughing, reenacting with bread figures the heroic battle the other would start with the aggressors. After a few hours and the fading of the pills' euphoric effect, she got up the nerve to admit she was worried. One bassist extracted from his leather jacket a small bottle he'd secretly stolen from the bar. He offered it to her, she uncapped it carefully as the bassist and the other bassist told the story of how they'd met, in a café identical to that one, but on the opposite coast of the Empire. The bassist worked in the kitchen and the other bassist delivered meat and cheese. Every Monday and Thursday, as they unloaded the blue bags from the truck, they talked at length about the new albums they'd bought and before long started making each other tapes with surprising mixes of songs. When the café owners bought a warehouse in an industrial district, the bassists began meeting there when they got off work, and walking together to the basements where the bands played. They teased each other gently whenever women approached them offering to buy one or the other a beer; in general, amid the monotony of all those guitars, amid the same verses as fifty years ago and the same choruses as always, they inevitably found a reason to abscond.

The bassists interrupted each other as they told her what happened next: someone had caught them in the warehouse, the one hadn't been able to stop the other from breaking a bottle over the head of a skater in a club, they shouted at each other and fought and stopped talking. The contents of the warehouse were moved from the industrial district to a new location on a now-abandoned touristic street. Long weeks passed without them calling each other. When the other bassist stopped working double-shifts, he started playing in Afro-Latino clubs; around the same time, walking home, the bassist found an amp and nearly-new bass in a dumpster and decided to take them, and proceeded to start writing songs. Until, a year and a half after they'd last seen each other, he strolled causally into the café and ordered something. He ate, paid the check, headed for the bathroom, but instead of turning down the hall to the right, he walked through the doors that led to the kitchen where the other bassist was working. They fist-bumped. The bassist wanted to know if the other bassist still had keys to the old warehouse in the industrial district. They met there that night. Holding a flashlight, the bassist asked the other bassist to follow him. In a corner, atop one of the collapsed shelves, all covered in dust, there should have been a tape the bassist had left for the other bassist the last time, a gift he never found. They began making their way through the detritus until the sound of a growl brought them to a halt. In a corner, a dark animal, a meter and a half tall, reared up on its hind legs, lashing its claws and gnashing its teeth. The bassist and the other bassist held hands the entire time. The cassette had vanished along with all the shelves, refrigerators, sinks, and containers in the old warehouse.

Back in the café, where they were now, so many years later, their story was interrupted when the vocalist and the other came in, arms around the four men who had insulted her and spit on the minivan. Beers in hand, they chorused tunelessly a southern church song and stumbled and fell; they crashed loudly into the one of the café's glass cake displays. The manager, seeing the glass on the floor, disappeared into a back room and reemerged with a shotgun. The waitresses egged him on to shoot, but three police officers appeared who had known one of the men since childhood and he took all of them back to his house. In the meantime, the other had come over to her and whispered, drooling in her ear, that it'd all been a misunderstanding, that the four men from the pickup had thought they saw a bumper sticker on the minivan for the band they hated most on this coast. The percussionist shoved him so hard he fell back onto the pieces of glass on the floor.

Now she was dozing again in the backseat of the minivan. On the floor, the bassist and the other bassist were playing chess. The truth was that cassette the one had left for the other in the old warehouse wasn't a mixtape of his favorite songs, they said. They were original compositions, six to be exact, that the bassist had specially recorded and dedicated to the other bassist; he hadn't had the nerve to tell him, he'd just left the tape on a shelf so that some random day the other bassist would find it. But now, it was lost forever. The other bassist sighed and kissed him.

Just then she woke up in the reclined seat of the convertible. She discovered the immensity of the sky of the Central Empire was a single cloud, it was going to rain. She looked at the clock on the dashboard of the convertible: it had only been four minutes since she closed her eyes. She tried to get up, but her arms were tangled in the heavy black jacket the vocalist had wrapped around her naked body. She shivered. He was sitting on the fender, burning some papers.

"Contracts," he said when he saw she was awake.

Then she pulled the lever and raised the seat, sitting up, and said that she'd thought it over, that she'd changed her mind. That she was going to stay in The Band. That, together, they were going to have a son and every night, to help him fall asleep, they would take turns telling the boy—she used that word—variations of the same fable.

PASTORTALE

|

Skinnybunny, Stinkat, and Bonehound jump. They jump, they run, they are hungry, and they are thirsty, but they hide because Accountant Carola enters with Scabrous Spouse, yelling at each other that the money, that the business, that the bonus, that the interests. They howl. One of the two dies; the other flees. Skinnybunny, Stinkat, and Bonehound jump when they see the body, they are hungry and they are thirsty; and yet, they are also hungry and thirsty for justice. What will they do?

II

They roll around in the humors mixed on the floor, they sleep one on top of the other on top of the other, they curl up, they stretch out, and they yawn: they have found a way to choose between justice and hunger and thirst. When one of them starts to drool too much, they bite, scratch, and kick each other.

Before proceeding, Stinkat, Skinnybunny, and Bonehound wrap the body in aluminum foil. Then they sit down in the light of the rising sun to demonstrate the different noises they can make with their bodies. Whoever can turn their noise into a sound, and that sound into music, and that music into awe such that it dispels the mood of despair, will have the solution they chose to defend prevail; nobody is convinced, but they proceed melodically.

Stinkat holds, with the oscillating murmur of the phlegm in her chest and the vibrato of her throat, that justice should be specific, and that—though it be a figurehead, an archetype, an example of an entire lineage they oppose—that specific body has done nothing to them, thus it is not just that they eat it and drink its blood. The others hold hands, they weep.

Skinnybunny argues, with the steady rhythm of his joints, to which he hypnotically adds the tapping of paws and jaw, that justice is a concept, and that, in order to conceptualize, the organism must first have attended to its biological necessities; thus the notion of justice is invalid when there is a body of which they can eat and drink, as they so need to do. The others dance, they applaud.

Bonehound points out, after a profound silence, in which the chorus of each of his hairs brushing against all the others becomes more and more perceptible, that justice is nothing but an arbitrary accord, a game they play among themselves, thus if one simply convinces a second that hunger and thirst are more important than declaiming convincingly before some unknown entity all the harm that body and its ilk have caused them for as long as they can remember, the third should submit to those rules. The others begin to sing.

The sun rises. Then Stinkat, Skinnybunny, and Bonehound leap all at once to snatch a coin they want to slip under their skin. They don't know it is just the aluminum foil attracts them, and so, all of a sudden, they find themselves on the ground scratching each other, hurting each other, because the place is infested with coins of every size and denomination. All riled up, it occurs to them to open the aluminum foil and let the plague of money depart with the body. And yet, would that be just?

|||

And that smell?

It's the smell of money.

And before Bonehound, Skinnybunny, and Stinkat can plug their noses, a squadron of Shoulderheads appears with whips, saddles, and wagons and jumps on them. They have them in custody when suddenly they notice the body.

And that smell?

It's the body of the Stupendous Spouse, shout the Shoulderheads; after days of tension, the kidnapping that has kept the public on tenterhooks has come to a tragic end. Bonehound, Skinnybunny, and Stinkat argue with them that no, that it wasn't them, that it was Accountant Carola and Scabrous Spouse, that with every death a mystery is born, and that the squadron is also participating in the search for justice and its lack.

But the Shoulderheads decide, instead of exploiting them, to take them to the dungeon. And throughout the interrogation they keep asking: and that smell?

First letter from prison
(Intercepted by a Shoulderhead and signed with a paw print that signifies
"All of us")

Now I shall do something we cannot tell the others about: don't distinguish the dungeons from the home, we are one and the same, and I swear to you on my veins the mystery of your empty signifiers is the key that allows us to survive the moments when we argued about justice, about representation, about community, about semblances, and we must know not only how to say no, no, and no, but yes, because if you leave behind our night and I am not one of the people with whom you would undertake an endeavor, please, let us remember the world and the sea and the other side. And the future?

V

Names? they interrogate.

All of us, all of us, and all of us, they answer. Then the Elbow-heads beat them; as many blows as the number of their presumed clandestine followers.

Then the Shoulderheads take note.

Names?

And for every beating, electrocution, burn, and submersion they suffer, in effect, a new collective rises in their defense without ever having met them.

We, we, and we, they answer in the cell. They are hungry, they are thirsty; but now their hunger and thirst for justice has grown.

Names?

They learn to make a single noise with their bodies.

Then the beatings stop; and, instead, they force them to eat bread and water, wine and meat, beer and vegetables, whiskey and caviar so they'll confess that they set off the bomb, that they robbed the bank, and that they killed Stupendous Spouse. At last, they eat, they drink.

Names?

Finally the Heelheads identify them: they are named Skimpy, Speck, and Bones. Is that noted in the court record? Are they written about like this in public? And do they thus go out into a world that from here onward has name, space, and time?

VI

Scabrous is leaving the 76th floor of a hotel that is also a ministry, embassy, food court, and train station.

She reaches out a hand to him—it's the only part of their bodies that retains a sense of touch—to enjoy free access to that lightness of spirit for the last time, now that the negotiations have been finalized: tomorrow they will sign the form that will bring about the privatization of everything disruptive, including their spirits and certain sensations that cannot be described.

In that moment, they look out the hallway window and see how in that last hour of the afternoon, the sun drops pristinely over a ravine.

What a beautiful place, she says.

Yes, he says.

We will even get that light to share.

But let's not deceive ourselves, continues Scabrous Spouse, as the doors to the elevator open and they disappear in the direction of subterranean 34: it's beautiful because we can look at it from a distance. We would never ever set foot in place like that. Imagine the hunger and the thirst of the vermin slithering around out there.

In that exact instant, the bodies of Skinbun, Stinko, and Bone-howl awaken; they are lying at the bottom of the ravine. They heard the conversation; all through the night and early morning they drag themselves in the direction of the government palace façade.

What is it that gleams, darkly, in their eyes?

VI

In front of the government palace, for centuries, there has been a lawn with the softest and greenest grasses ever trod on. It's called Petitioner's Square. And for centuries it has been the place where the Shoulderheads and the Heelheads stock their munitions, catapults, tanks, drones, and clubs. The Kneeheads, even, play tag there.

Dawn breaks on that historic day.

Eight groups of eight hundred have gathered together to make their lips vibrate synchronistically in front of the government palace. Nobody has ever been able to enter Petitioner's Square without a uniform, but that morning, the hum of their lips grows so great that its expansive wave sends the fences flying, the patrols scatter, and the satellite cannons implode forever.

The eight groups of eight hundred begin to advance through their own clamor.

The first column shouts that, in the name of Bonebunny, Stinker, and Tombkat, they would not allow the privatization of everything disruptive. That everything belongs to everyone.

But when Bonebunny, Stinker, and Tombkat drag themselves into Petitioner's Square, nobody knows who they are.

Better that way, they say. And they surrender.

And yet, the ninth group of nine hundred, the rearguard that is entering the government palace recognizes them. Someone decides to detonate all the bombs.

Something explodes; it isn't their bodies. Now the lawn is hard clay, pollen, shrapnel, pieces of palace.

Who will the Elbowheads imprison for this unjust attack?

VI

Flank, Bringsomething, and Unjudge the Wise don't even groan anymore, trapped as they are in the high-security prison.

The Heelheads, who toss the international chef's latest experiment through the little window once a week, spread the rumor that there is nothing in that subterranean cell but a statue, a bust, and an equestrian figure.

Until one night, the Ghost of Justice pays them a visit in their cell.

It comes in the form of an about-to-burst drainpipe and the sound it makes through the wall tells them the following tale: The train arrives to the village. A little boy and a little girl—brother and sister—are sitting together, and out the window they note the details of the station as the train comes to a stop. Look, says the little boy, we are in Damas. Silly! the little girl replies, can't you see we are in Varones?

The next day, the warden, Accountant Carola, explains to the public that the prisoners made their escape when the drainage system collapsed.

Why, then, does the story spread among the Heelheads that, on that night, they heard a peal of laughter so powerful it shook the high-security prison to its foundation?

VII

Second letter from the underground
(Delivered by six whirlwinds and signed by a paw print that signifies "theothers")

You speak of justice. You act in the interest of justice for every man and every woman. Your deity is just, justice is your deity.

But it is unjust that justice be of more importance than the other needs of those who stand beside you. It is unjust that justice be of more importance than the need of the other person who stands first so others can stand too. It is unjust that justice is a paradox and not a concrete fact: justice does not exist and Justice does not exist, but we cannot not have it.

How can you ever truly come to smell yourself, hear yourself, see yourself, touch yourself except with mirrors—which have an owner—if not through the bodies of those who stand beside you?

VIII

Injustice happens, it happens.

Only thus can the new government of Scabrous Spouse explain to the remaining four why the valley now is farm and the hill is fort; the sea, port; the desert, saltpeter; the grassland, highway; the glacier, reservoir; the forest, lumber; the river, runoff; the lake, shipping, and the city, bank.

The rest of the eight hundred are now theothers, too worn out from the hammer, the spade, the scythe, and the keyboard to ask again why, who is responsible for all the injustice.

Until one day Skinnybond, Comfortcat, and Saint Bonekiss arrive to the waiting room of the new government skyscraper, dressed in suits and shinning shoes. Skinnybond shows his device to Scabrous Spouse, Comfortcat waves her rag, while Saintbonkiss begins his prayer so the President can complete it.

We are here to bring an end to injustice, they say in unison.

The President applauds, rises, shakes their hands to welcome them to the government. Because nobody knows them, he says to his secretary, Accountant Carola.

What will her demand be when she finds them out, and what the response of Skinnybond, Comfortcat, and Saint Bonekiss when they enter the subterranean room to discover that from inside a glass coffin the body of Stupendous Spouse, a stuffed animal without paws or maw, is the one in charge of everything?

VIII

And yet, Ms. Cat, Don Skinny, and Mr. Saintbone do not attend the feasts at the skyscraper palace. Nor do they go on international tours; they limit themselves to making reforms, while in cabinet meetings Scabrous Spouse defends them against accusations of being technocrats, populists, lobbyists, fasters, to explain once more to the young ministers—who spend time in the government before obtaining lifelong economic posts—what the miracle by which Ms., Don, and Mr. have governed for thirty years consists of: television, telephones, internet, free sports for everyone; subsidies for basic services; the organization of festivals, parties, and dances. Of employment, education, housing, and nutrition policies, not a thing.

Then comes the famine.

The famine was not anticipated.

The progeny and their vermin take to the streets, camp in the squares, and burn the fields. The other eight hundred, the other eight hundred thousand, the other nine hundred, the other thousand thousands—already old, already fat inside—let themselves die of starvation.

At an emergency government meeting, Accountant Carola opens her eyes at last and finds Stinkat, Skinnybunny, and Bonehound standing before her. She thinks they are smiling, but realizes it's just a sneer, a silent growl. Accountant Carola recalls all she has lost to years of popping pills: a ravine, the sea, three creatures of the night. So she and Scabrous take advantage of the foggy night to embark on a permanent diplomatic mission to the great beyond.

As that last sun rises, a bedraggled mass of millions stands before the ruins of smoking mirrors that once were skyscraper, palace, garden, forest. They cry out for a piece of bread and a drink of water.

The burning sun rises.

Out of the ruins emerges a ridge that is a hill, a hill that is a volcano. And a cat, a rabbit, and a dog emerge from the crater; with the help of millions of other paws and hoofs we push a glass coffin, gilded and on wheels, down the last liturgical ramp. We make ourselves legion: never again will we let some salivating thing turn into ration, into reason, into nauseating money. We crowd together, carefully we open the coffin and, justly, we eat.

The choreography needs a silence. He, the boy, stole twelve chainsaws from the logging company before he was caught. He, the singer, felt the electric shock from her, the other, the bassist, and the other bassist's instruments in his throat, in his perineum, in the nape of his neck, and in his gums every night.

He, making his escape, began to write names on a stone, for he knew the wind would erase them. One of the names was the name of The Band. I am he. She, the other, the bassist, and the other bassist had to choose a stormy night.

For every erasure that my eyelids carry out on the screen, a series of words that I do not write on the blank glass is regained: pëllü, silence, electricity. That was the order in which the old mother taught him, the boy, to speak.

Only a strong wind can touch everything at once.

He, the boy, threw himself into the other's arms. She, from her hospital bed, smiled at the three of them, exhausted. He came over and, instead of kissing the newborn on the forehead, planted a kiss on each of his eyes. What name are you thinking of for the baby, she answered, the other answered, he answered.

He, the singer, discovered the figure of his twin outside his cell window was climbing a hill, entering the boarding house, crossing another threshold, arriving to the room she had rented in the apartment as an adolescent. He, making his escape, wrote names in the sand of an immense and stormy beach.

I, on the other hand, no longer remember what is sound and what noise, what is nasality, and what those mouths are that vibrate above me.

He, the singer, on the farewell tour asked that the penultimate song always be followed by a pause. Each of them would dedicate it to whomever they wanted, pëllí, silence, memory, chainsaw, and so every night the guitar paused, the keyboards stopped, the basses ceased thrumming, the cymbals and drums were left untouched, trading places, superimposing.

He, unlike me, heard in each of those silences the deafening roar of the chainsaw cutting down his tree and all the other unreachable trees simultaneously.

I am he and I can touch him, the boy, again, but only with my eyelids.

6.
CORRECTION

The choreography needs a silence. Though the enormity of the great stone could be framed within the camera lenses of the tourists, who started taking pictures as soon as they stepped off the bus, the other found it hard to look at. The warm air and the midday sun made him not think twice about abandoning the line and the flashing cameras and the marveling exclamations and disappearing along a gravel path that meandered upward between craggy boulders and golden grasses. On his device, at full volume, he listened to The Band Project album that featured multiple drummers, but couldn't rid himself of the memory of his mother sighing into the phone, when he told her he'd joined the Anti-Empire.

He stopped humming and sat silently in the precipitous shade of two veins in the rock, removing the water bottle from his backpack. He had climbed without rest until he was face to face with the great stone's summit. From where he was, there was no trace of the bus or the tourists. He was taking off his shoes when he started to lose his balance, just managing to catch the backpack: the bottle went bouncing down until it was swallowed by the altitude. The other sat down on the hard surface, stretched out his legs, took a deep breath, and began to drift off to sleep. And yet, he repeated to himself, he could no longer feel the shiver the song he was listening to gave him before, the vibrations of the suspended synthesizer, hanging there, waiting for, from one moment to the next, the mentor's deep voice and the piercing guitar to weave in and out, chasing each other, until finally coming together in the chorus of drums. He couldn't hear anything. The damp heat and the pain in his back woke him with a start. He looked instinctively for the water bottle, lamenting aloud having lost it. He stared at the huge stone, balanced atop a tiny base, and it made him feel vulnerable. I'm having a nightmare, he thought. He opened the device, blew on the laser, changed the batteries; it played again, but he wasn't listening. The stone was still there, he couldn't see it without color and without the possibility of touch, on the brink of weighing more than his body could ever bear, rolling, enduring, and shattering when the tiny pedestal of his body gave way. Everything would break apart, but the monumental rock would remain unfazed: another thousand years of dust, elsewhere now, in another position, another light and another shadow.

He removed his headphones. Of course, he'd put them in wrong that morning: the right in the left ear, the left in the right. Suddenly he heard pebbles scattering, thumps, footsteps. A young man about his own age, tall and dark, appeared before of him. Dressed in worn-out jeans, boots, and no shirt, his bare torso contrasting with the long wavy hair that fell to nape of his neck. The other greeted him, but got no response. He saw that the young man wasn't carrying a backpack, bag, or water bottle, only a small Bible in one hand, and that he snorted like a horse as he proceeded up the stone path. That was the first time the other saw his vocalist. Then he shut his eyes and fell into a deep sleep, like he hadn't slept in weeks. The mentor's baritone faded, then his father's shouts, the shoves, and the door slamming for the last time. Finally, there was just the stone, alone in all space, solid, immutable until it was shrouded in a kind of fog that also contained a silence in which he didn't know his name or what language to say it in, whether his mouth was full of a pleasant liquid or if he no longer had mouth or nose or hands or eyes. Hours later, a man with a long gray beard woke him. The sun had gone down and a light rain was starting to fall. They took a shortcut down together, through beer cans and bags of food detritus, flies and fruit peels. The man with the beard told him the tour guides were looking for him. He really preferred the language of the Empire, he confessed, it felt better in his mouth than the anti-imperial hybrid. He talked nonstop: he told the other that he worked for the ex-priests, organizing a festival of ancient choral music; that he was also an ex-believer; that he had come to show the stone to some friends and had caught a vandal in the act of defacing the patrimony—that's what he called the stone. The other came to the vandal's defense, asking the man if he hadn't ever done graffiti. No, no. But the vandal had taken out a pencil and convinced him to write some biblical trivialities at the base of the stone, the man with the beard told him. Some verses no one will ever read, he said, and suggested they hop the tourist fence so he could show him. The other declined, saying he was tired. To tell the truth, his vision clouded over just thinking about getting anywhere near the stone.

The choreography needs three. He, the singer, on tour, tried to ignore the lights in his eyes, the throbbing ache around his waist, and the deafness from all the sound checks, because despite everything he could feel how she, the other, the two bassists, the hired wind sections, the drums and the bongos and the maracas and the gong, all played along with him.

I am he. He, who can no longer be touched without gloves.

She formed a chord with her fingers, let them fall one by one onto the cymbals, warm, embracing the next chord. The other waited for her on his string. The drums thrashing in his temples, on the other hand, announced that the masses, there, ecstatic, would have to go out into the streets and destroy public property if the President remained shut away on the top floor of her palace, unlistening.

He, the star, heard nothing.

"The thrashing in the trees, boy, is not there to hide you," protested the old mother when he, chasing the kawellu and the blind chicken, smelled in the thunder the trucks that carried away all the dry wood, and asked her for protection.

He, the singer, every time that the thrashing announced itself, gave a single cough. He would prepare by clearing his throat. He would intone an inaudible bronchial hum, until, with electricity, she and the other played the signal simultaneously.

He, the hills facing the sea in his cell, stared out until he saw whether or not it was the other who came to her apartment so that she would open the door, after spending the day motionless in front of her drum set. And yet, in the blink of an eye, the streetlight on the corner went out, the power cut by the bomb blast, the thrashing that the other prisoners gave him, waiting for his voice. His scream.

I, on the other hand, reduce the brightness of this screen and eliminate the names three by three: my blinking, her fingers tracing the nape of my neck when she stays up late reading the score in bed, her touch on the backs of my ears and her index finger tangled in what's left of my hair. The screech of the other teaching the boy a succession of keening notes, yes my shining sun, on your string. A chord.

He, the star, wanted to continue the tour because that night they were going to be heard in the language of the masses, and that would give him back a scream that would allow him to remember his true name.

"Each bird of morning opens its beak because it is on its branch," the old mother said before throwing a stone.

"A third is needed to know if this is a call, a break, a warning, an enticement, or a response to one who is far away." A fourth, she answered in her island, peninsular language, from the hospital bed with the boy in her arms looking up at him and looking up at the other. A fourth.

I, on the other hand, blink open my eyelids just once and three names, three characters, three times are replaced in quick succession.

5.
CORRECTION

The choreography needs three. The handful of individuals who paid a fortune to get seats at The Band's reunion concert had to contain their impatience for close to ten minutes. From their positions, the reporters witnessed how, in the first row, the imperial minister's face drained of color, how the neatly trimmed, contract-signing fingers of the proprietor of all the bread began nervously tapping on the seat in front of him, how the made-up mouth of the bald starlet from all the ad spots fell open with the passing minutes and wouldn't close, because the frenetic bass drum that opened The Band's latest anthem never came.

The three of them had appeared on stage with only a wooden harp and a tube organ, no retina-filling digital close-ups, no three-tiered orchestras or eco-political rants, no apocryphal verses or on-screen explosions. And then, with a nod of the vocalist's head, a grinding hydraulic engine raised the neoclassical façade of what had been the municipal theater, so the concert was suddenly out in the open air and the one hundred seats were immediately surrounded by hundreds of students, workers, the unemployed, assistants, advisors, protestors, grocers, new arrivals, dogs, and girls who at that hour rummaged through the dumpsters of the old neighborhood's high-end restaurants. The finance secretaries of the Anti-Empire took the moment to light up their water pipes, because it was all starting to make sense: the prohibitive cost of the exclusive tickets for The Band's only reunion concert had been used to rebuild the façade of the old municipal theater in such a way that, minutes before the opening song, all the people in the streets had congregated there.

That had been the only condition the percussionist, the vocalist, and the other had stipulated when the mentor's wife had proposed the reunion concert. And, in effect, it allowed thousands of unanticipated attendees to all at once connect The Band's multiform discography with the enigma of their first toccatas, with the ideological saturation of their recent productions, and with the battle royale that exploded in the park at that summer concert when their breakup had been deemed consummated: the effect was rage. The Band made music out of rage; what rage, shouted a barefooted man. Just then, in the sky, the roof open now too, an enormous hologram appeared, showing documentary footage of clashes between fans and police at the festival in the desert, at the exit to a classical music festival in the old northern capital, during the predawn hours of the new year along a stretch of beach bordering the jungle, and in front of the parking garages at Estadio Popular, in counterpoint with the audio of the shouting matches he, she, and the other had at those final press conferences. From his seat, a supreme judge of the First Hemisphere coughed, then a group of haute couture designers raised their glasses; these were the previously agreed-on signals for a detachment of military bodyguards to encircle that faction of elites in a protective ring. The swelling chants of the masses, interrupted by the helicopters, could be heard over everything. The show hadn't even started.

"What the organizers want," someone said over the radio, from the trenches, "is for the rage to spread from one side to other."

Then a great spotlight drew all the tension to the proscenium. For the first time at one of The Band's shows, the vocalist appeared on the stage fully clothed; for the first time, he remained quiet, stony, distant; for the first time, his exhortations were not heard as soon as he set foot in front of the microphone: he started to dance, convulsive, until his arms tangled with his foot and the masses gasped in unison as he fell to the ground. At the same time, the other began to finger the harp and it became clear, from the low resonant notes echoing off the façades, the lights, and the concrete, that she was playing the tube organ with her feet. A cold fog was creeping over the elites and the masses, getting everyone wet; there were thousands now and you could barely distinguish one from the next. Maybe it wouldn't be through pure rage that they would come to glimpse the totality the combination of all the songs of The Band Project, Cueros, The Band, and the different members' various solo albums aspired to; the appearance of the two bassists, the percussion section, and a symphonic choir in the pit that used to separate the audience from the musicians, had the effect of elevating the hundred thousand privileged, greedy voices that intertwined, that identified with one of the many melodic vocal lines of that long and famous song, and that kept on singing. The seconds expanded, as the voice of each individual came to understand itself in the voice next to it and those voices in all the other voices there, intoning, uncanny, a harmony that wasn't just a promise, that wasn't embodied in a leader, in a faction, in a party, or in a government, but in an excessive, disciplined, complementary force, all one: the sound of all those bodies all at once. The minister's muscles flexed at the same time her tendons relaxed, a kind of animal horde had taken over the old municipal theater and was moving docilely in the direction of something new, in a language not spoken by diplomacy: sound in itself. The minister didn't recognize it, though she was a polyglot;

neither did the owner of the subway system, nor the biotech wunderkind, nor the crown princess, nor the most-lauded writer, nor the oil baroness, nor the old pharmaceutical speculator, nor the game's fair-haired heartthrob, nor the oligarchy's public relations managers, nor the last great athletes, nor the two hundred most influential, accredited reporters. Nor was it the non-verbal language of artistic composition. It was a promise, nothing more, but there was nobody left to say what it meant as a collective experience: the chorus of voices would be swept away, with all the bodies of the audience, by a rhythm that would carry them not to that same place—there, where they lived—or to an entirely different place, but to the inside of an accumulation of palpitations, perspirations, afflictions, exertions, plenitudes. With that heartbeat, each individual would begin to dance asynchronously yet simultaneously, in different ways and at different paces, but aware of the person beside them and of the groups as a whole, such that even the possibility of dissolving into a harmony would transcend exclusive generalization.

The vocalist, on his feet again, just another voice in the chorus of thousands, snapped his fingers in front of the microphone to precisely mark the introduction of the next rhythmic layer just as two gentlemen of the oldest bloodline, whom nobody had even noticed in their seats, could no longer bear it and, with a clap of their hands, they gave the final signal. Then the military bodyguards about-faced and stormed the stage, while the police, armed with batons and machine guns, advanced on the masses. One individual, the whole multitude, saw the flash of the rifle butt strike the vocalist's neck, a second before the blackout and the stampede and the massacre, his mouth open wide as he fell, his vertebra catching the corner of a stair, his voice still echoing through the feedback, down into the pit.

The choreography needs repetition. He, the singer, preferred the sound of his own voice to the look he got from her, from the other, from the masses at the last show, all asking him not to do what they expected him to do: not to jump into the pit, to limit himself to singing and dancing.

I am he, and yet.

Only my pupil lets me repeat a sound that could be my nose blowing, even if it is only in writing and I have no nasal cavity other than the respirator.

He, a word in itself insufficient at keeping a warning from sounding on the screen, because for the last nine minutes my eyelids have stayed open.

"The flame doesn't burn deeply, the coals of burning branches are better. The embers," said the old mother.

The light of this screen doesn't burn.

He, running through the neighborhood with his brother, stopped to listen to the repetitions of the rain on the zinc roofs. He, in his prison, got charlie-horsed over and over until the spasms took him elsewhere.

He, the boy, slept in a dry wash in the summer.

He, hidden from the security guards, took refuge in any house where a fire burned in the winter.

"A sound, among the majority of anti-imperial peoples, moves not just the bodies of us animals at its whim, but all else that might receive the soft breath of wind.

"If you perceive music as a pleasing accord of sounds, if you listen to it just for fun and dance to it as social entertainment that provides a modicum of physical exercise, before long you will feel separate from the music, from the sound, from your body, and from everything that can perceive the softest breath of wind."

He, after hearing the sound she made in the bathroom, thinking she was finally alone with the boy, heard nothing else for weeks.

I am he, and yet. A voice inaudible through the warning siren that sounds, because I haven't moved a muscle in over half an hour.

5.
CORRECTION

The choreography needs repetition. The deep and resonant bass, the sustained snares, the solid cymbals. The almost-imperceptible guitar in the background as counterpoint. And the voice of a woman writing letters to a lover in her mind, a lover whose name we'll never know, as she drives along highways outside the Empire, the morning sun on her shoulders. A saxophone begins to mimic her vocal lines. The woman removes her dark sunglasses, lights a cigarette, and then the clapping and chanting of the religious congregation of a lost town in the Central Empire comes in, to give poignancy to the list of objects the woman recalls putting in a hotel incinerator: a packet of tobacco, some worn-out pants, a photocopied novel, a small flask, a bottle of pills, and a toy ring.

It's "Imperio (parte I)," the song that opens one of the surprise records of the just-ended decade. In the liner notes, the names of the performers don't appear anywhere, just a list of instruments, photographs of barren landscapes, and hand-drawn sketches of twisted faces. Who are Maria y Las Primas? Taking into account the brass section's precision, the melodic enthusiasm of the bass and string parts, as well as the commercial production, you would think they were just another teenybopper band. But then there are the restrained drums and the innumerable guitar effects evoking artistic ambitions that would drive an antiestablishment band from any town in the Anti-Empire to try to escape an unpredictable schedule of bar, school, and train-station gigs.

What's even more confusing is the fact that this album was released on the imperial label Gdmld, previously devoted exclusively to reissuing The Band Project's complete discography. And yet, there is a connection between the mentor's introspective citations and the exuberant longing of Maria y Las Primas: the fact that they resurrect the elitist tradition of the concept album for a wide audience. But whereas the mentor set up each album of The Band Project as a response to a different capital-Q question for cultured ears, Maria y Las Primas offers a collection of songs about everyday working life, imaginary letters a woman writes to amuse herself, as she moves from her bed to her job and back again. On the commute, her voice lyrically explores the contradictory nature of social relations: the vocalist savors the banal fact of driving her car in solitude down indistinct highways, but can't help thinking about the woman waiting for her—and whom she cheats on with other men and other women just by virtue of not being with her—in some metropolis; her lyrics are evocative, but wouldn't have such resonance if they weren't accompanied by an ensemble of rhythmic virtuosos. Maybe the musicians aren't really related to that singing voice, but their heartbeats pulse in similar times, like what happens with any group of people who live together long enough.

The single, "Pëllü", is, with its three minutes of lists, orchestral hooks, and bass lines that evoke the early days of disco, an example of how love songs need a corporeal relationship between two people to carom off the people surrounding it, in order to be isolated; if a meaningful encounter has an echo it's because somewhere there's a cavern. The vocalist enumerates a series of personal objects her lover leaves in her room every time they see each other, things she spends her entire monthly income on and uses as pretext to see the vocalist again; the series of personal objects is punctuated by the chorusing of the Primas, who respond to Maria with descriptions of remote landscapes, canyons, ridgelines, plains, hills, ravines, valleys, deserts, mountain ranges, yet also remind her of the existence of a beach, the ruins of a city, an enormous limestone cliff, the erosion of an ancient sculpture, a tree with flowers so heavy with pollen its branches graze the surface of the river, the squeals of pleasure of two children as they swim in the sea for the first time. That call and response is what it is to be a family, that coming together summons all of us to hum its succession.

The choreography needs audience, someone to witness its movements.

I am he, the other, she. And yet, the room and its operations and the voice of the boy are the only sounds that echo back to me.

I am not the other, she, he.

She, he, the other only came to know each other around a bonfire, in its dying embers.

4.
BONFIRE

That last night the flames illuminated our faces, because the fire was made with dry sticks from the labyrinth the girl with the dyed hair had apparently been building in the birch forest, though most of us knew she just liked breaking off branches that appeared dry, that looked to her like stumps of coiled paper, which she could make use of back in the city as material for some neighborhood art installation, and that on the pretext of tracing the projected space for her labyrinth, she really spent the afternoons at the residency hunting those mushrooms with the pure red cap and no white dots, though the assistant had to impart that latter clue, and we thought she did so a little too late, and that's why the girl with the dyed hair had a fever for so many days, because she took it upon herself to boil and consume any red mushroom she found, never offering any to anyone else, and, the second night, she began arguing about whatever random thing, first with the quiet owner, then with the photographer, then with the drummer, and then there was nobody left to warn her it's not about the redness of the mushroom cap, the brighter the color—the more striking its brightness, the more exposed to the sun its location—the more dangerous it is for the person who consumes it; also it's not about boiling it until it secretes a particular color and foam, like a soup, rather, in the preparation, there is specific, traditional knowledge, one of the performers told us during that first hour of the night while we were gathering firewood, there, in the middle of a clearing where a couple seasons prior another resident had built an archway out of vines, branches, morning glory, wire structures, a portal to who knows where, we laughed, and the dancer confessed that she had almost gotten some shears and come out and cut it down in the middle of the night, because of the harm that huge sculpture seemed to constantly be inflicting on the birch trees, maybe that was why they had retreated in that part of the forest and a clearing had opened where, one of the owners told us, just a year before had been pure dense vegetation, because the trees were being forcibly trained and to what end, if the plant considered it a piece of embedded metal, useless even for its vine, an accident a few strange human animals happened across twice a year, and the intervening object itself had begun to rust, and she found the diagonal orientation of the trees disturbing, what was the point, she almost howled, while we picked up one piece of firewood too many to carry back to the bonfire, because the screenwriter had convinced us to put—among the lowest coals, sheltered by stones and slow-burning wood, near the roots, vegetables, and sausages—some homemade sweets that smelled foul when the flames touched them, so rank that we ran off to find some aromatic fuel for the fire. The three of us set off. That last night of the artists' residency, the path to the cabin grew even darker, because in that place, at the end of summer, as we'd been warned, there was a fog that rose and got inside you, and the truth is we were kind of scared of getting separated, moreover nobody could remember if we'd stashed the bottle inside the bag of weed or the bag of weed inside the bottle, so when we managed to get the key into the lock of the door, convincing ourselves whatever it was that was coming from the forest was nothing more than the cold whistle of the wind on the napes of our necks, whatever it was that on other nights—and when we got to the light switch we realized the power was out in the cabin again, after feeling about with our hands in the pantry, in the closets, between the towels, under the rug, into the shower, where there was still hot water—had forced us to ask how sure we were that he was grabbing her, that she was groping the other, that the other was putting his fingers inside him and her at the same time, we were barely able to stand, smoking more, laughing again at some comment about the song that choir girl was singing, religious she, religious he, religious you, around the bonfire when the food began to smoke; since there were no plates we used the last napkins and it occurred to us to go to residency's sauna to get newspaper for the fish the second performance artist brought back after a whole day spent at the nearby lakes with the owner of the horses and his son, but when we opened the sauna door, we found the drummer with one of the owners, already steaming, so we stayed quiet, to better hear how the assistant asked us where we thought life came from, if in our countries there were more interesting words for the spirits of the place, *wangulenes*, ancestors, demons, guardians, presences, tremors, terrors, residents, *djins*, souls, storytellers, cramps, sleepwalkers, winds, doubles, creatures, others, flames, extraterrestrials, déjàvus, cumbajas, don't laugh at this, the local artist said to us in the exact moment the fire went out, went out on its own, and we could've sworn there was no wind in the dry night at the residency, at that hour, the truth is we were taking a piss a short distance away, behind the third cabin, and in the fog we—she, he, the other—became entangled when we came running back, holding hands. The performance artists took advantage of the darkness to run off with the bottles, and we had no choice but to give chase. Laughter echoed through the trees, through the forest, and then, even, along the path that, according to the local music, was covered with frogs at that hour of the night. We followed them until we passed the sandy marshes, the cattails, and suddenly emerged from the fog and found ourselves on a beach. The performance artists shrieked and threw clods of dirt at us from the dock, challenging us to follow them as they got into the boat.

3.

A CUERO ON THE SAND CALLS
TO A CUERO IN THE WATER

We stuck a full leg into that place where the swamp began. Some of us weren't even wearing shoes. Legs sinking into the thick mud, up to the knee in some cases, we arrived to the place where the backwater ended and the tide began, eddies, sandy banks now, you take a step and fall, you take another and get up, and yet no matter, because we ran until we could grab ahold of the rotten, wood edge of the dock or the boat, where the cold of the steel column touched our legs and our fingers spread as we pulled ourselves up, our fingernails digging into the boards, we didn't let the performance artists get the oars and they moved away, taunting and heckling, some of us were even wearing pants, boots with long socks, because here, at the end of summer it is already starting to get cold, no matter, some of us had wrapped our legs in strips of gauze while smoking and staring at the bonfire, because of the chill in the air; the area hospital had donated the surplus supplies for our art projects, and we stitched the strips of gauze together with purple thread, and when we climbed into the boat that night, those who didn't quite make it, because the bottles were slipping out of their hands and they were carrying pieces of grilled meat they were trying to keep from getting wet, grabbed ahold of the gauze to keep from being left behind. It was inevitable we'd make some error, water swallows any food you offer it, especially under a full moon, which became visible when the wind began to blow and the fog lifted, and in the reflection some of us were able to make out the gleam of the rusted nails in the boat from which the performance artist threw back at us what, you remember, pumice stone, pieces of wood, rubber balls, beans, sugar cubes, leftover stale bread from when we mixed and kneaded and shaped a human figure, and put it in the oven, and the man inflated, the limbs rose and the eyes popped open beneath their lids, the mouth's lips swelled, and under the lips the teeth turned brown and under the teeth a tongue moved, a throat swallowed, and that night we took off running too, until we realized we'd gotten separated and were lost in the forest. We tried to find our way back, we were lost for hours, some of us had stayed behind, paralyzed there in the kitchen, until we took out the butter, spread it on the bread figure, and ate him before he could grow any bigger, before he cooled, we couldn't wait for everyone, so on that last night some of us ran across the sand until its denseness released us and then, without knowing how, we had found the beach. We were carrying drinking glasses the sea snatched away from us immediately, nothing easier than filling a glass with salt water for such a strong midnight wave, and the moon looked red to us, red but not with light; the artist who didn't know the language and the assistant and the owner and the second owner, even the photographer, who had already been there quite a while, recalled what the locals had told us, about what it might mean if a red moon were to break up that night's dense fog, and we suddenly found ourselves on that one beach nobody had emerged from the forest to find for many seasons;

ever since the strange human animals arrived, the birch trees had taken it upon themselves to hide the nine exits. Then, exeunt. One of us began weaving in the boat, not with the gauze that guided us through the swamp, and how was it possible all that thread she brought stayed dry, oh how her hands moved in the night. There were ten of us sitting together in a half-rotten wooden boat, at high sea. We had taken off our pants, shoes, blouses; a soaked pile of clothing drifted toward us, back in the direction of the beach and we couldn't stop laughing, we wouldn't be afraid to imagine what'd happened to the girls, pass the bottle, it'll get better, and when one of us reached out her arm, another opened her mouth, and when another stopped laughing because something was wrong with the keel of the boat, because it was breaking down, because more water was getting in, because we were tipping over, one of us even had to untangle her legs, which had gotten wrapped in seaweed, another was trying to take off someone else's boot she was wearing on her right foot, better pass the bottle, the matches, we exhaled in silence and hung our arms, shaved legs, and heads over the wobbling edge, intertwined we dried ourselves in the wind, warm at last, damp, but then, when it dawned on us what that wind and that red moon breaking up the dense fog at that hour at the end of summer meant, the assistant said since we had eaten the bread man, the spirit of the place would no longer appear to us, maybe that was why we had finally found a way out of the forest and onto the beach. One of the performance artists pointed at something dark in the distance and threw a seashell at it, something we couldn't see and that convinced us the totality of the night had concentrated in a single point, so we started to kick as if rowing, but the wind grew cold, the swell broke, and the boat finally collapsed beneath us, what else were we going to do when the floating column exploded into salt, the thing was that out of all of us she, he, and the other were the only ones who knew how to swim, so it is likely the rest never made it to the boat and it is even more likely the three of us just stayed there drinking on the sand.

2.
BEACHING

That was all, we swam back from the wreck of the boat against the currents that pulled away from the shore until our feet touched bottom. Drenched, panting, our clothes hindering our movement, we let ourselves drop to the sand, pale in the light of the moon of that last night.

We were only three: she, he, and the other; you fell asleep, we said; we threw sand in your open mouth and you snored, no, I was dead after all that swimming, I need first aid and laughter, more sand to my open lips, just as the spark leapt to the stack of firewood, we'd protected it with our body from the hands of the others and managed to get the flame lit, just as the wind had stopped blowing from our mouths, eyes, holes, orifices that are not the same but work anyway; we were showing each other the entrances as well as the exits, touch here, see how they don't look alike but work just like in the bonfire, our clothes were spread out to one side and we lay down on top of them so we could bite and cling to each other and share space, shivering, crying out with and without laughter, engorged where the wind wouldn't blow, try this, suck on that, viscosity like we'd never known, and yet; we found a way to swim with the full bottle, don't ask how I held on; tension, reflexes; the first birdsong and as the red moon vanished, glimmering golden on a distant hilltop we'd never seen before, speaking without saliva at that hour, fluid without body, I don't believe you. Yes I do.

We believe you. We spoke only in whispers, at the volume of the crickets and frogs, softer than the wind which is all one but everywhere. Whereas, the three of us, more than conversing, were explaining to each other, in voices that didn't sound anything like dialogue, the reason why it wasn't the first time we had spoken. We saw her face, his face, the other's face, confronting each other, the imaginary memory illuminated, the moon had been concealed by the fog, and we wondered who we were now.

We heard all of that, along with the sound of the sticks burning down to embers, the embers taking flight as ash, the ashes scattering in the wind. We heard our lives but not our stories. Hers, his, the other's, and without moving we dried ourselves. We placed the last of the ashes inside a seashell we'd found there, where we lit the bonfire, a single, translucent seashell that we sealed shut.

I.
THE SPECTER OF WHAT CAN ONLY BE TOUCHED

By then, we were warm. By then, we could leave the clothes where they were, sit with our legs open in front of the bonfire and listen: it was daybreak, the new day, and we saw each other's faces, who are you that you want to know so badly whether he was with her, whether she was with the other, whether the other was with him, whether all three together is possible, and if asking even matters, we said before listening to each other.

The other started to make his lips vibrate, pressing them together so all the flesh of his mouth released a deep note just as the first sunbeams slanted through the trees, across the lake, toward the sea, alighting on her hairless arms, which she began to rub, because the moment had given her chills. And yet that rubbing gave way to light palm taps that, with each slap, after a slight pause, punctuated the depth of the other's sound, and before the fluty note of the first birdsong, getting ahead of it, he began to fill the spaces that she left open in the other's vibration with a wail, a shrillness that ascended and descended when she, using her free hand, attempted to move a stick in the bonfire to make use of the side of the coal, and didn't let it go, but instead attempted to counterpoint each beat with burning wood, with her palms and his fingers, with the sounds—who are you, why do you want to know so badly what language we did it in?—with the syllables the other began to string together into a repetitive sequence that broke down when the first shadow appeared as the sun rose in the sky. She joined in the exchange of cries that came together with all the birds singing at that early hour, with his exhaled responses, with the sound the other's fingers made as they tapped in sync with everyone's lips, and it was harmony, artistry, sand that began to throb on the taught skin of his chest time and again, a singing drum, theme of three, our song, music, they said. And they listened.

"Listen," she said to them. "It has been a revelation for me to get to know you during this artist residency. I didn't expect to make music again, much less work with strangers and with men; but this song we just played, does it belong to anyone?"

"Listen," the other said to them. "I think it has been important for the three of us to have agreed to come to this artist residency, to leave behind the inertia of The Band, the problems of commerce, the sexual tension, the custom of property, the superimposition of couples, the fantasy of the band, the vanity of authorship, and, at last, to make music together again; but this song we just played, doesn't it belong to the three of us and so, when we record it, won't it be the central theme of our comeback?"

"Listen," he said to them. "I don't know who the two of you are and I don't care; don't tell me where you came from or what brought you here, or how we came to make music together around this bonfire; I don't want to know about your childhood, about your parents, about your neighborhoods, about your youth, about the people you've been with, about your jobs and your art projects, about your shortcomings and your accomplishments, about your original and present cultures; but this song we just played, doesn't it belong to an expansive life that has just begun, to a mass of elements that only have a vibration in common when they touch, whose masses combine in a way that is not just one, but many yet to come, and that, up close, is composed of atoms, cells, tissue, organs, bodies and, at a distance, is composed of cities, towns, villages, hamlets, rivers, beaches, and mountains that won't belong to this place, to this seashell, to this bonfire, or to this residency with its strange human animals, music that doesn't belong to the listener or to the reader, but to the person who can imagine it never existed and understand it nonetheless?"

By then, we were already dry. By then, we could have gotten dressed, but we didn't.

The choreography needs melody, day-to-day it was my fantasy there would be company.

A beat plays that stops, that wakes me up.

I am he.

The sound envelops this body from inside. The organ repeats the theme. I, on the other hand. I, on the other hand.

He, the boy, holding hands with the old mother, asked why they didn't let him blow his nose into the hollow stick that was part of the instrument and why his shrill voice couldn't carry on her repetitions.

He, the singer, dismissed the second and third voices the other suggested for the most melodious part of the album that would bring them the fame and fortune and give them an excuse to break up. The other didn't elaborate, just reincorporated them as percussion.

She and the other, on the other hand, harmonized in low voices in the hospital, on a chair and in the bed.

"What a melody it might be, more than a kind of company, a way for me to be?" he bandied and didn't look pleased, nor could he, when he heard what they were singing.

The old mother, on the other hand, boy, she swatted him away so he'd keep the necessary distance.

That word, melody, didn't exist in the language of the old mother, or in that of the old mother's mother, or in that of the old mother's mother's mother. He would keep his distance.

He would blow out of his mouth until his nose, eyes, and ears blew too. I am he and if I were singing I wouldn't try to speak.

0.
THE GLEAM IS ONLY IN
THE PUPIL OF THE EYES

The choreography needs melody. A girl was running an electric razor along the nape of a woman's neck in one of the salons on the university square, observing through the mute windowpanes how four patrol cars pulled up on all sides of an obese man wearing a gardening dress and a hat, pointing a rifle at some foreign executives coming out of a bar. The obese man had smiled a second before the police took him down in a hail of gunfire; the girl saw this on the television in the salon. She was interrupted by the sound the boy made, sitting in one of the armchairs by the door, kicking the rug to the rhythm of her clipping scissors, opening and closing. She had seen him before, the girl thought; the boy seemed to be singing to himself without opening his mouth. When he looked back at her, she realized that because of his headphones, he probably hadn't heard the noise out in the street.

"Gotta go," the boy said, looking away from her, getting up and trying to walk with feigned agility, catching his headphones as they fell from his ears as soon as he opened his mouth, almost tripping and falling.

The girl shrugged. Before the door to the salon closed, it seemed to her the boy had said something else, words that hadn't fully registered, in a language she didn't know. She stood, looking out at the street again, the sirens, the masses confronting the helicopters and the cameras, the obese man's limbs poking out from under a silver tarp, the ambulances. Then she remembered some particular words: she remembered the boy's full name and that in high-school choir class he was usually two spots to the right of her in the top row, that the first time she had caught him by surprise, staring at his mouth, as the two of them sang the lowest notes of the a capella version of the *éxito primaveral* in the neighborhood; she remembered she had understood what the boy said in that other language, minutes before, to the woman accompanying him, the woman whose hair she was preparing to dye in that exact instant:

"Don't cut your hair," he'd said. "It'll grow out again anyway and they'll recognize you."

The woman, whose hair the girl now trimmed with the electric razor, had, until then, sat completely still, eyes gazing past the mirror. But she turned around when she heard the boy's voice and, disregarding the blade of the electric razor, got up from the salon chair. She tried to say something, but saw the boy had already run out the door into the square; her voice caught in her throat and she swallowed. She turned back to the mirror, smiled, and sat back down. Her phone vibrated incessantly in her hand. The girl couldn't help but notice the caller on the small screen: "Hospital."

The memory entered her mind of how, on the street at a stoplight, in the backseat of the big car of an executive who paid her for two weeks of full service, she had sat up briefly and had seen a very attractive man walk by. She was struck, staring at him. She blushed when she realized not only did she know who he was, but she knew just how he smiled, the particular way he stretched out his arms when he woke up in the morning, the proud inflexion in his resonant, imperious voice when he asked a question, and that little wrinkles formed along the edges of his mouth when he was tired. The executive who was paying her pushed her head back down; her situation—that she needed to get a different job—became painfully clear to her when the executive looked out the window and sighed:

"Look, there goes that actor from that show."

From that moment on, the girl knew without question who the boy was, as she smiled at the woman in the chair in the mirror, applied the final ointment, finished cleaning the base of her neck, dabbed behind her ears with a cotton swab, damp with a little mineral water, offered her a product she turned down, charged her, gave her her card, wished her a pleasant afternoon, and watched her push open the door that opened onto the university square, where she got into a taxi. Of course she remembered who that client was now, the salon's cosmetologist had been showing her pictures of a drummer who painted her body to match the other members of The Band for their shows.

As soon as the clock struck five, the girl left the salon at a run; three new male clients had requested her by phone. But as her pace slowed with each step, it became clear to her she had joined a mass of people that was taking shape on the west side of the square and there was no room to run. She had to cancel the dates on her screen, regretting having to waste what she'd made that day at the salon on data fees. She was dragged along by the mob for hours, all the way to the big park where the victory of the immigrant woman in the presidential elections was being celebrated. The girl watched dozens of feet trying to push forward, she had been looking down at the pavement ever since, on one street corner, some skinheads had reacted to her surgically-enhanced body and grabbed her around the waist and, to her surprise, pulled a blue T shirt printed with a crucifix down over her torso, and she couldn't take it off, because her hands were too busy keeping her upright amid the arms of all those strangers, a throng of skins pressing against her and propelling her forward, and finally a metal gate, a stage, spotlights in her eyes. A roar of amplified instruments and a multitude of voices singing and dancing convinced her to look up at the stage, and she realized that The Band's vocalist was approaching her, he sang to her from a few centimeters away, but she could barely see him, because of the spotlights shining in her eyes.

She remembered too that, for choir class, they had decided to practice that spring's popular song all weekend, in order to perform it at the Emancipation Day civil ceremony. It was late one Saturday night, their throats burning, because it was their responsibility to carry the melody with their lips and not with their breath. The boy tried to show her for the zillionth time how to project her voice, but they ended up kissing and going at it in the showers. When they finished, she—who in some ways was still a he back then—felt a pain somewhere deep inside, deeper than her intestines, and she tried to explain to the boy it wasn't due to his lack of experience or the hormone patches, and then they got a kick out of taking pictures of the colored stains in the urinal; during the previous two weeks one of them had eaten only asparagus and the other only beets, so during the last months of school, in addition to singing medieval hymns in unison, they ran together to the bathroom. The colors didn't dissolve easily in the water that streamed down the white ceramic. They didn't mix either. Amid the masses, looking up at the vocalist and the percussionist, whose hair she'd had the honor of cutting that very afternoon, the girl remembered how, when they were smoking together for the last time on the school rooftop, the boy had taken her by the hand and told her he would be moving away with his family, with The Band, to a remote and inaccessible location in the Anti-Empire.

"Do you think the world is really ending?" she'd asked the boy.

"Of course it is," he'd answered with a sigh. "Your world, but not mine."

And as she wasn't going to be able to free herself from the mob of fans who were using her strong shoulders to climb as far as the security guards who repelled them with cattle prods, the girl slipped one hand inside the T-shirt and wiggled out of it and started swinging it around in an ascending motion up her other arm, until the shirt flew toward the stage and hit the vocalist in the face. She didn't care about this concert, the force of the knee against her back, the expression on the face of that figure photographed thousands of times and broadcast on all the screens of her city to the point of nausea. She cared about the light in her eyes; all she could really see was the back part of the stage.

"Life here begins many times," she'd said to the boy later, hanging out in the school's back stairwell. And she let the boy put his hand on her aching groin.

The boy's face was no longer familiar to her, but he recognized her too, that evening, from his position backstage. He wasn't so familiar anymore, and so she began to feel attracted to him as a potential client, smiling at her from a distance. That was her memory of him. She was more worried the light would reveal the sweat on her skin; that it would dilate her pupils too much and that wasn't healthy, she thought, just before she fainted.

The choreography needs a rhythm, a rhythm that isn't moving.
  I am he. He is that.
  That is the beat. The beat is distant.
  I, on the other hand, your shadow and I.
  What was your shadow doing at night in the waves?

1.
WHAT WAS YOUR SHADOW DOING AT NIGHT IN THE WAVES?

The choreography needs a rhythm. That night, from the third-floor balcony of the embassy, the straight line of the southern horizon yielded, lost its coordinates, and in the end was just the shadow of a cloud advancing toward the city and sweeping over the sea the vocalist and the other were staring out at, barefoot, toes turning purple, in silence, passing a bottle they'd stolen from the bar at the banquet. And smoking.

"I read it somewhere, in an imperial library, I think," said the other: "'The oceanic feeling.' I can't forget that phrase. And likewise, I've never lost that feeling of the smell of the brine and the wailing of the gulls and the children carrying little buckets of saltwater, the footsteps of a couple pressing into the sand, and the sun falling on your face, but you're in the sand dunes, you can't see the water or hear anything, you don't feel warm or cold, all you feel is the constant murmur of the ocean, though your head is submerged in your own moisture and maybe in sleep, a calm that comes and goes, the ceaseless crash of one wave over the next, the dangerous waves way out on the open sea, you know; a state in which you escape yourself and you smell the salt, but at the same time you're alert because at any moment the tide might come in and sweep you away, the breaking wave drown you, you stay calm, your eyes are closed and you're far away yet touching everything because the water extends as far as your eyes can see and, even though you keep them closed, you still hear it. Do you hear it? I read something similar in another book; the book of an old man who was celibate, yes, but why when all the priests are locked up and their horrible church is illegal. The celibate man talked about a southern visitor belonging to his same organization who went through all the towns seeking a new kind of experience, someone enlightened in the ways, or a colleague who might find in song, in drawing, in multicolored stained glass, a piece of that thing so many people talk about and claim to know, and that nevertheless doesn't exist anywhere, except in what they were selling every Sunday. The visitor explored the rural byways until he reached the sea; he walked along the coastline and finally came to where the last tongue of earth jutted out into the water. He spent days and nights on those cliffs, staring out at the water. Until one day a saint appeared to him. For two days they discussed the oceanic feeling. By the third day, the saint was ready to throw himself off the cliff."

The vocalist touched the other's arm so he would be silent. He leaned into him and with difficulty got to his feet and walked over to the railing of the balcony, where he stood, looking out. Early in the morning, days before, in the center of that Anti-Empire city, outside Banco del Pueblo, the other had run into a bearded man strumming versions of themes by the mentor, by The Band, by Maria y Las Primas on his strings. He cashed the check he had stolen from the ambassador and invited him out to lunch. And though he and the vocalist had spent the last seventy-two hours together, improvising sounds and harmonies with guitar duets on the rooftop of that building (until the security guard showed up), the vocalist had barely said a word to him. And now he raised his hand, holding the bottle, pointing at a spot in the distance: the cloud had definitively enveloped the sea so earth, water, and sky were a single block in the night, a block that included the concrete of the city, the walls of the embassy, the invisible trajectory of the bottle the vocalist threw toward the tops of the park's tallest trees. The other couldn't remember what argument the celibate man had used to convince the saint not to jump off the cliff, to stay there with him instead, looking out at the open sea, for another day, and then the next one, and two more after that, until he got used to remaining alive. That was the most important thing, he thought, just as the vocalist pointed at a break in the clouds that revealed a white shape out in the water, maybe a boat, a rocky outcropping illuminated by a lighthouse, the glow of all the city streetlamps reflecting off the wall of fog. His fingers had been swollen, not anymore. He heard the sound of the vocalist vomiting in the bathroom, minutes before the hand of his old friend had been pointing not at a spot on the perfect line of the horizon, which was now reforming, but at the figure, growing larger, determined, striking, of a woman who tried and succeeded to scale the great wall of the embassy. He took a drink from another bottle he'd found in the pocket of a pair of pants on the floor and looked back toward the bathroom, the door slightly ajar, where the woman was cradling the vocalist's head over the toilet. Sitting on the floor, she had offered them something to smoke that she'd brought in her pocket.

"What did that celibate man have to offer apart from saving the life of a saint?" she said through the smoke, through hard consonants and soft vowels that betrayed her origin in some suburb of the disappeared Empire. "And those of us who aren't saints, who aren't celibate, who aren't men staring out atop some sublime cliff, we just fucking deal with it. Whereas once upon a time, even farther to the south, there was an old mother who didn't worry at all about the existence of the ocean. She had knowledge of trees, of illnesses, of small animals, of one horse, of the climate, and of the two young boys she raised. They looked like twins. Throughout her life, the old mother had only known mothers, the mothers of her home and other mothers from far away, until one day the two boys arrived. The two boys are the two of you.

The vocalist wiped away the bile with a sleeve, gave a little cough, and went unexpectedly to curl up, eyes open, beside the percussionist, who continued to speak. He moved his mouth as he listened to her words, but made no sound other than a few soft moans.

"One night, the old mother had a nightmare unlike all the others, she grabbed the two boys and took them up to highest boughs of the their favorite tree. Sitting down below on a stump that had appeared in front of her house the day before, she waited for the logging company's security guards, contract in hand: a *kultrún*, her drum. The guards came with first light, uniformed and armed by the central government. The old mother was waiting for them with a percussive song that went on for hours and terrified them because in it they glimpsed the decrepit, sick old men they'd become. They shot her twenty times, used the chainsaw on her, and after the rainstorm that blew in on a freezing wind, that same night, they shot each other. Those two surviving boys told this story in front of some functionaries of the central government, who didn't listen, because that same day the first drone strikes of the imperial expansion were falling in the southernmost reaches."

The other, the guitarist, realized he was starting to hear music, a rhythm, a massive musical structure, as the percussionist seemed to stop talking, to concentrate on caressing the eyes of the vocalist. He went to sit beside them, but stopped a half-meter away and didn't know how to get any closer but by offering his lighter, while in the distance they heard the rumbling of hundreds of vehicles hoping to reach the highway before there was nothing left.

"The twins would blame one another for having sung in vain. Until they sang again," she concluded.

Then, as the sun rose, they began to applaud.

The choreography needs pause and movement.
  Something is still missing before we can go up and play.
  That, over there, is that a seashell or a stone?

2.
THE OTHER STONE,
BETTER KNOWN AS
THE HOUSE OF BONES

"The choreography needs pause and movement," she said, turning down the volume on the film she was projecting.

Beside her in the bed, propped up on pillows, the vocalist opened his mouth and blinked at the same time. She wondered how long it'd been since the expression on his face hadn't been sad, while trying to hear who it was who had arrived to the house. It was just the boy and the other arguing, she intuited; after the laughter broke off, one of the two left with a slam of the door.

That night there was a lot of wind. Is there anything physical like the wind, something tactile you cannot touch? What is a draft of air, if not a superstition? She remembered when he playfully formulated questions like that, in a low voice, beside her, in the enormous bed of a hotel in the Empire, that time they weren't allowed to leave until they accepted a payment from the intelligence office. Among the inane requests the vocalist made to exacerbate the tension, was to demand they open the sealed windows only to, two hours later, beg them to close them again, holding his sweaty arm away from his body, because he dreamed the drafts of air could give him a backache. In the *qullasuyu* film she was watching, the bodies began to dance, not caring about the tanks rolling into the square in front of the government palace.

She turned up the volume with the remote control, starting as she began to nod off; she didn't want to fall asleep yet, so she turned toward him, stiff amid his cushions, to wipe away the drool with the sleeve of her old sweater. Throughout the night, she'd wake up and run a finger around the outside of his mouth. She'd clean the snot from his nose and the goop from the corners of his eyes too, but now, this time, he reached out his stiff hand—that pale and thin hand that so often had clung to her own or to the microphone—and grabbed her. She didn't understand how he was suddenly able to move, why he squeezed her palm until the blood from the wound formed a streak. In the film, on the screen, nothing of which to speak. Across the window, a crack, a break. Hush now, not a peep. A farewell blowout. The vocalist rehearses: it's time for me to go now. Out on the beach, she and he and the other burst apart. The dream makes her faint—black out.

"Now it's time to dance. Everything in its place."

A bit of the dialogue between the characters in the film woke her up. She tried to grasp what was happening, who was saying what, but the masses had turned into a *diablada* that had overrun and swallowed the tanks.

"Now play," stammered the vocalist, sitting up in bed.

She sat there looking at him. No longer fixating on the lines of his wrinkles or his motionless cheeks. The cushions and pillows were on the floor. She wasn't trying to understand the disordered movements of his pupils anymore, but seeing him speak, in complete contradiction to all scientific diagnosis, it dawned on her now he wasn't supporting his back against any surface either. That stiff hand, which was clinging to hers, tried to caress her.

"Now play."

He hadn't said those two words in the imperial language or in the language of commerce, not in Chezungun or the language of the rabbits or that of the peninsula or that of the island or that from across the sea either: the sounds were completely foreign to her and yet she'd understood them anyway. The vocalist didn't want to write his autobiography with his eyes. He wanted to sleep. She wept.

A door slammed.

"We've got some wind," the other said when she wasn't expecting it.

He had been watching the two of them snore from the bedroom doorway. He was holding three glasses of lukewarm water in his hands, he didn't move until he heard her stir. He took off his shoes, his tie, his suit, and got into bed with them.

"That boy of yours can't be convinced that a thing will never again become what it once was if it is determined to be transformed. He's still looking for the girl, the stylist, in The Man. I told him memory can be operated on, too, now. He took off."

She was waking up. Sleepless, The Band's percussionist amused herself by pressing a series of buttons on the remote control; the projection changed format on the wall, bulging, the soundtrack dropped and out of the crowd of choreographed bodies the voice of one actress emerged. The wound on her hand had stopped bleeding. The Band's guitarist saw another scar on the opposite side of her hand she'd never shown him before. She let him look at it in the half-light. The vocalist appeared to have fallen asleep among the cushions, at last; maybe the three of them would finally rest in front of the mass that had dismantled the attack with their dance, they wouldn't pick up their instruments to help.

"What language is this choreography in?" they asked.

The door would open and close one last time, pause and movement.

The choreography needs correction.

NOTE

This novel includes paraphrases from texts by Ana Mariella Bacigalupo, Michel de Certeau, Lydia Cabrera, Lawrence Hayward, Thomas Mann, Chantal Mouffe, Jacques Lacan, and Manuel Manquilef.

Carlos Labbé, one of *Granta*'s "Best Young Spanish-Language Novelists," was born in Chile and is the author of eight novels, including *Navidad & Matanza* and *Loquela*, and two collections of short stories. In addition to his writings, he is a musician and has released five albums. He is a co-editor at Sangria, a publishing house based in Santiago and Brooklyn, where he translates and runs workshops. He also writes literary essays, most notably on Juan Carlos Onetti, Diamela Eltit and Roberto Bolaño.

Will Vanderhyden received an MA in Literary Translation Studies from the University of Rochester. He has translated fiction by Carlos Labbé, Edgardo Cozarinsky, Alfredo Bryce Echenique, Juan Marsé, Rafael Sánchez Ferlosio, Rodrigo Fresán, and Elvio Gandolfo. He received NEA and Lannan fellowships to translate Rodrigo Fresán's novel, *The Invented Part*, which won the 2018 Best Translated Book Award.

OPEN
LETTER

WWW.OPENLETTERBOOKS.ORG

**OPEN
LETTER**